SCOTTISH SHORT STORIES

1987

Introduction by
Iain Crichton Smith

COLLINS
8 Grafton Street London W1
1987

William Collins Sons & Co Ltd
London · Glasgow · Sydney · Auckland
Toronto · Johannesburg

First published 1987

Love Story © Kirkpatrick Dobie 1987; *The Boiled Egg* © Rosa Macpherson 1987; *Betty Corrigall* © George Mackay Brown 1987; *Miss Deft* © Erik Coutts 1987; *Vlamertinge* © Lorn Macintyre 1987; *The Spider* © Jane Webster 1987; *Territory* © Ian Rankin 1987; *American Dream* © Maureen Monaghan 1987; *Norika* © Peter Regent 1987; *Redundant* © Andrew Cowan 1987; *Georges Minh* © Jackson Webb 1987; *Schwimmbad Mitternachts* © Ronald Frame 1987; *Optics* © Christine Adam 1987; *Washing the Blankets* © Maeve McDowall 1987; *Life Support* © Guy Kennaway 1987; *Round the Square* © Philip Hobsbaum 1987; *Sunday* © Astrid Wilson 1987; *Take-over* © Naomi Mitchison 1987.

The Publisher acknowledges the financial assistance of the Scottish Arts Council in the publication of this volume.

BRITISH LIBRARY CATALOGUING IN PUBLICATION DATA

Scottish short stories, 1987.
1. Short Stories, English—Scottish
authors   2. English fiction—20th century
823'.01'0894II FS   PR8675

ISBN 0 00 223196 4

Photoset in Linotron Baskerville by
Ace Filmsetting Ltd, Frome, Somerset

Printed and bound in Great Britain by
Robert Hartnoll (1985) Ltd., Bodmin, Cornwall

CONTENTS

INTRODUCTION

If it is not true that everyone has a book in him, certainly a large number of Scotsmen and Scotswomen appear to have a short story in them. There were 350 entries this year, and the task of selection was as difficult as ever. The day of course will never come when three judges will be unanimous in their choice, but it was surprising the number of short story titles which appeared as common on three different shortlists. Still, there was much hard bargaining after that. And that is as it should be. The taste of the judges is catholic; we were searching only for quality.

This is not the place for a long disquisition on the Scottish Short Story, its characteristic strengths, weaknesses, etc. And naturally we haven't unearthed a pristine cache of Chekhovs. However, it might be worthwhile for those who intend to contribute in the future and who failed in the present to categorize to a certain extent the unsuccessful entries. These tended to be one or more of the following: (a) naïve in the sense that they were not artistically articulated; (b) derivative; (c) inconclusive or obscure in the denouement; (d) lacking in narrative 'grip'; (e) pedestrian in the writing, underwritten, or overwritten.

It might also be worth mentioning that one of the characteristics of the Scottish Short Story as represented in this series, over the past few years, has been its setting outside Scotland, and the fact that it has incorporated characters who aren't Scottish. There are French, Japanese, American and Vietnamese overtones in this collection. There is nothing unhealthy in this – it would be odd in a rapidly contracting world if it were otherwise. The day of the couthy Scottish anecdote masquerading as a short story is over.

However, we return in the end, as in all good short stories, to the human not the geographical content. There are stories here about love in its many manifestations, some exceedingly bizarre; indeed, if there is a common theme then it is this. One would wish in particular to pick out 'Love Story' by Kirkpatrick Dobie, which is beautifully worked in terms of both life and literature. The connection between these, and between imagination and 'reality', was a theme to be found in many of the stories submitted but it can be a treacherous one. 'Love Story' however is exquisitely wrought, with its fine autumnal tone. And it would be invidious not to mention 'Life Support' by Guy Kennaway, a powerful and unusually daring story, so tactfully handled that that which might have been distasteful becomes a glowing paean to a love which is manifestly true but manifestly not 'romantic'.

There is, we think, an interesting mixture of 'names' and of the hitherto unknown in this collection. It is clearly important that an anthology such as this should bring the anonymous freely in from the wings, and it does so with much pleasure.

Finally, it cannot be stressed too strongly that this anthology should be considered on its merits, and not as a document mirroring a 'deprived' Scotland. There were of course some stories of this nature but the majority of them did not qualify, for reasons simply of artistic competence. 'Relevance' on its own does not guarantee a good short story. It is not the job of a short story writer to be a social commentator, unless he wishes to be; his job is to write the short story that is in him and do it as well as he can. The stories you will find here are about real emotions such as love and jealousy. They are, we think, the best of the entries submitted (we say this with fear and trembling, since judgment, especially about art, can never be infallible). However, in the room in which we toiled there was no sound of axes being ground. All we can do is hope that you enjoy the stories we have selected.

IAIN CRICHTON SMITH

LOVE STORY

Kirkpatrick Dobie

If only she could get herself to concentrate it would be material for a novel, a love story unlike any ever attempted, the best yet, and all the better because true.

She would begin, she thought, with the bombshell of his declaration. She had heard – or rather, half heard – his emergence from Papa's study, and waited, as it were without awareness, for the sound of the outer door. It had not come. Instead had come a tap at her own and what was to follow had flashed on her like lightning.

It had been preposterous. She was a famous woman – for she *was* famous, though it was an effort to remember – and he only what her father was soon to be calling 'a hundred-a-year curate'. Papa's anger had known no bounds and there he put himself in the wrong. Besides, fury was no compliment. He ought to have known her better. She had said as much when she told him she would write a refusal.

But that had not been enough. He had written, too, adding insult to what must necessarily be painful enough to any man. It had forced her to write again for she could not, in justice, let him think she shared her father's opinion. She could not let him think she despised him. Her letter had been formal, even cold, and no more than a note, but it was inevitable it should seem in some small sense encouragement. She had realized this but saw, too, it could not be helped.

From then on she avoided him but could not avoid hearing how he scarcely ate or slept, and in church she could see for herself how haggard he was. There had been relief when he resigned and when, because there was difficulty filling his place and he attempted to recall himself, relief again that the attempt failed.

Papa had made it a condition that what he called his presumption should never be repeated. This had been refused and for that she rather admired him. Soon after, it was heard – for in the village everything was heard – that he had applied to become a missionary. It seemed he meant to put half the world between them. So much the better, she had thought, though less would have been enough.

It would need careful writing for she would have to make it clear that Papa was not an ogre. He had, just before these events, had a slight stroke, the effect of which was to increase a natural impatience. Passages of this sort – bridging passages – were difficult to do and if not done well had an air of insertion. For the rest, the main part, she had no fears. She could see it all in sharp little scenes and the marvellous, never-to-be-lost-sight-of thing was that they required no invention. For it was all true. This time it was all true. When she had been ill – very ill – it was the only thing she could hold on to. It had been a strong rope drawing her up from a well of blackness.

Perhaps the best scene would be herself at communion, pale but self-possessed, and he, dark, sensual – no! she could not use that word – but brooding, looming over her like a thunder-cloud, offering the bread – the bread of life – but breaking down as he did so and hardly able to recover himself. Unmanly drivelling, Papa had called it, but *he* had not been there. On those who were, the effect had been different. From that moment opinion had begun to swing his way. He had never been popular. He was too alien, too abrupt and self-contained, but now it seemed his pain had touched their flinty Yorkshire hearts and reached their even less accessible pockets. For there had been a presentation – a gold watch – and that, too, had been without precedent.

It must have been about this time she had written to Ellen: 'I may be throwing away the purest gem.' It had been a jest. The truth, as she had gone on to say, was that they had nothing in common and she was not going to marry out of pity. He was a good enough man who respected his calling, but that was all. Literature was nothing to him, not even the literature of the Bible. He was limited, even in the little they had in common –

the Sunday school and the parish. He had no imagination.

She had told Ellen she did not dislike him. She had, in fact, never disliked him. It was rather that she did not notice him. He had, from the first, been glanced at and dismissed. When she put the local curates in her book he came off best simply because he made least impression. Now, instead of indifference, was embarrassment. It was not an improvement.

Yet embarrassments and oppositions made a novel. They were the frictions that gave a story warmth and colour. Here, nothing need be manipulated, for events had taken their own path, written their own story, never flagging, never repeating themselves, never losing the thread, yet taking turns and twists that, though unexpected, were yet acceptable to sense.

All this she had told Mrs Gaskell, and how there had come the last of many last moments when he would hand over the deeds of the National School. They had to be delivered to Papa in person and she, of course, had kept out of the way, hearing him depart with nothing but thankfulness. This time all doors had closed behind him, and yet, listening in relief, it occurred to her there had been no sound from the garden gate. 'At this,' she said, 'and remembering his long grief', she had ventured out, meaning, if he should still be there, to wish him brief Godspeed. 'It would,' she had said, 'have been no more than courteous, not to say Christian.' But she had found him in anguish, 'sobbing as women never sob'. It had been shocking, terrifying. She could not tell what she said. She had gone to him as she would have gone to the victim of a collision on the roads. It had been necessary to tell Mrs Gaskell this and a great deal more, for by then she was meeting him – meeting him in fields and lanes, in secrecy.

Even to kind Mrs Gaskell it had been difficult to explain how this came about. It had begun, she said, with his letters. From Kirk Smeaton where, waiting word from the Missionary Society, he had taken temporary refuge, he had written sometimes twice a week, and she could not bear it. It was not that he wrote well. He did not. He could not express his feelings. His letters were dull like himself, but that made no difference. To her they were intolerable for they brought back with exquisite anguish those she had written years ago to Constantin Heger. 'So long as I have hope of receiving news from you I can be at rest,' had been her words, 'but when day by day I await a letter and when day by day disappointment comes to fling me back into over-whelming sorrow ... I lose appetite and sleep. I p ne away.'

At his sixth she had given way but only to write with all the force of sober conviction that he must abandon hope. It should, like so much else, have been final, but he had replied, begging her to write again if only to repeat what she had said, and in his humility and self-abasement she had seen herself again.

Yet it was madness. She did not – could not – love him. Her estimate had never altered and when they began to meet it remained the same. To Mrs Gaskell she said that, though she appreciated better his true worth, the disparity of taste, inter-ests and intellect was too great. No respect could bridge it.

'But you do not feel this so much when you are with him?' said Mrs Gaskell, and she had replied that when she was with him she did not analyse her feelings. 'But you are sure of him?' And to this she said yes, adding that he was incapable of dissembling. 'He could not if he tried,' she had said.

To write this part would be difficult. One had to be precise about a denouement, especially one that involved a *volte face*. Readers expected it. Yet she thought she could not *be* precise. She was not clear enough about it in her own mind. It might be best not to attempt it, but merely to state the outcome, and leave to imagination what occurred – the *salto mortale*.

Ellen had been against him and offered good reasons, but Mary Taylor, writing from New Zealand and perhaps from more experience, poured scorn on them. 'Duty!' she had writ-ten. 'Have you not then a duty to yourself?' And Miss Wooler too, and surprisingly, had been on his side.

But the choice had been hers and she could not make it. Apart from anything else, she was too old. Indeed, when she looked at herself in the mirror she marvelled at how any man could desire her, especially a man to whom her one talent meant nothing.

Left to herself she would have let time solve the problem, as it had solved the problems of those whose tombstones she looked on from the parsonage windows, but with the curious quick instinct that seemed to possess him in everything that concerned her, he had chosen this moment to write to Papa asking leave to renew his suit.

In the face of her parent's astonishment and rage she had been obliged to confess and defend their meetings. She was not in love, she said, but should be given time and opportunity to confirm her feelings. This was a respectable man, his proposal was honourable, he had a right to be heard and that was all she asked. She would not be carried away by anything. She was not a young girl.

But debate had been increasingly difficult. As her father raised his voice she had had to raise hers. It was unseemly, embarrassing, especially with servants about, and always, overriding everything, the fear he might have another stroke. In the end it had come to exhaustion, to tears and flight.

Had she been writing as a novel all she was now vividly remembering, this would have been where it ended, except for an epilogue or, as in *Villette*, an ambiguity. For the truth was, she had no confidence in happiness, could not believe in it, could not give herself to it. Life had been her teacher and she had been always too much an apt pupil. But upstairs, face in pillow, she had become aware of battle continuing. To her ears, muffled though they were, had come the harsh clarion voice of ancient faithful Tabby, demanding of Papa, amongst other things, if he meant to kill his daughter?

She had hardly been able to believe it. No one had ever defied Papa. His authority was unquestioned. It had to do, of course, with Tabby being deaf. She did not realize she shouted, nor could she be argued with. Papa had not attempted it. He had retired, slamming the study door. Yet it had been no more than minutes before he emerged to say he would oppose no longer. Charlotte might do as she wished.

There had been no explanation. Some new factor had entered his consciousness, or suddenly everything had been seen in a new light. Whatever it was, whatever name one gave it, she knew the source. It was love. Love had accounted for his opposition as now it accounted for its withdrawal. Love was a very strange thing, stranger than anything she understood when writing her books, or even when writing to Constantin Heger. She had thought then she measured all its heights and depths. Now she knew better and knew it to be inexpressible. It was too vast, too comprehensive. This book that was beginning to shape itself would be an attempt, but would go only a little way. Yet she must try, must rouse herself, for to travel that small distance was more important than anything else in the world.

There was not much more to think about. From then on, everything had proceeded as in life it never did. Even Papa had begun to see advantages. True, he had not come to the wedding and there had been a flurry when it seemed there would be no one to give her away. But it turned out that the Prayer Book did not specify sex and Miss Wooler was able to take his place. It was something, she thought, that might be enlarged on. Suspense, coupled with useful information, gave body to writing. It focused attention and raised the author, for a reader was always, to some extent, aware of the author. Moreover, it distanced events from each other to give an effect of time passing. And reader and author had always to be conscious of that. Miss Wooler at the altar would be a symbol of something that lay near her heart – the right of women to be acknowledged for qualities unconnected with their sex. It was delicate ground, but if ground for anyone, then surely for a writer, for who else was there to express such claims? Who but a woman writer of accepted standing could insist that women be treated as responsible human beings?

From that point it would be easy to return to her main theme for, standing in her father's place, Miss Wooler would represent also the struggle and compromise that had brought her, desperate yet half-hearted, to a decision. Half-hearted, for even on honeymoon she was writing how it was too much to expect that character and principle should be accompanied always by congenial tastes. She felt herself grow hot – hotter – as she remembered that. And yet, it did not matter. If she had not followed her heart or had heart to follow, he had, and had had enough for two.

Sick though she still was, she knew she had never been happier than at this moment, still feverish, but without a care in the world. Even at Thackeray's lecture when the great audience, the élite of literary London, parted ranks for her to precede them, she had not been so happy. Indeed there had been no happiness. There had been only elation, nervous and unreal. She had returned with relief to the parsonage, bare as a bone and silent as the graves outside it, the clock's ticking heard everywhere except when the wind drowned it.

Love was security and it was only now, when she possessed it, that she understood how much it had been her need. She must have missed the mother she could not remember. What she remembered was Maria and Elizabeth and how she had clung to them. They had all clung together. When as children they went out on the moors they held hands, the six of them, like a string of beads. Anne had been only three ... when Maria and Elizabeth returned in dreams they were distanced. She had not been able to understand that.

In Ireland, Arthur's relatives had proved to be of consequence – it was like him to have made nothing of that – and he himself remembered and respected. 'I trust I feel thankful to God,' she had written, 'for having enabled me to make what seems a right choice.' 'Seems,' she thought now. 'Nay, I know not seems!' Later, it had been: 'When I see Mr Nicholls put on gown and surplice I feel comforted to think this marriage has secured Papa good aid in his old age.' It was better, but cold. It was unworthy.

There had been a party in the schoolroom when they got back: singers, bell-ringers, and Sunday school teachers, five hundred in all, and Arthur's health was proposed as 'a consistent Christian and kind gentleman'. She, who only weeks ago had left in lace mantle and white bonnet, so fragile that it was said she looked like a snowdrop, was returned in health, so changed that in their faces she saw herself as almost beautiful.

But it was hot. Too hot to concentrate and that was bad, for thoughts drifted, and out of the heart proceeded fornications, murders, thefts, covetousness, deceit, lasciviousness, evil eye, pride, blasphemy ...

15

They had not accepted God's world but had created their own. It had begun after Maria and Elizabeth died and she wondered if that was why they came back cold and disapproving. If so, it was no more than to be expected, for pride, anger, adultery and the rest was the history of the secret kingdoms. Emily had written:

> And am I wrong to worship where
> Faith cannot doubt nor Hope despair
> since my own soul can grant my prayer?
> Speak, God of visions, plead for me
> and tell why I have chosen thee.

If that was worship it was not Christian worship and Emily had not died like a Christian. She had died like a Queen of Gondal. Anne had been Christian and even Branwell had expired with 'Amen' on his lips to his father's prayer. But Branwell had been in terror. He had taken a knife to the Black Bull one night, meaning to kill the devil. It was the kitchen knife – a long-bladed carver. Grundy had told the story – no doubt with embellishment – but in essence it would be true. For Branwell also had rejected God's world and hell was what he exchanged it for. God was not mocked. Whatever a man sowed he would reap.

But if Branwell dreaded hell, Emily had learned to live with it. Tumbled out of heaven she had waked sobbing with relief on Haworth moors. Hers was a terrible book and it was lucky Arthur could make nothing of it – nor even, for that matter, of Anne's. For Anne, too, was suspect. She seemed so simple as to be transparent, and certainly what she wrote had moral purpose. That could be granted. But the books were shocking. There was too much acquaintance with evil. It was the same with her poems. Indeed, they were worse, more revealing. What seemed mild and pious was, when you looked closer, almost criticism. 'A Word to the Elect' was an example. It seemed innocent; but if you faulted the elect were you not faulting God? Was it not God who made them elect? And there could be no two opinions about 'Oh God, if This be All!' That *was* criticism.

She had loved her sisters. She had loved all her family, even Branwell. She loved Papa. How could it be otherwise? But it was the curse of the writer's art to probe and estimate even nearest and dearest. Thank God there was nothing in Arthur to probe and it was thanks to him she was forever delivered from the vivid evil life that made decent men seem dull and inferior. God had been good. She was wife to an honest man who loved her and whom she had come to love. Perhaps, after all, she would not write this story. Arthur would not like it. He did not like to think of her as a writer and he had been so good, so kind. This illness had brought out the best in him and to that extent been almost a benefit. Now the fever was abating. Already she had begun to eat again. Soon she would be well. Papa was provided for. Everything was safe and Arthur had been so kind, so kind, so good, so patient ...

And Arthur Nicholls had been all that. Of his great love there could be no doubt. Charlotte had made no mistake there. Seemingly content in a second marriage, he had yet, years later, told a friend his heart was in the grave.

Charlotte herself, waking in these last hours, had found him at her bedside. He was lost in prayer and for a while his words made no sense, then her mind cleared. 'Oh, I am not going to die, am I?' she said. 'He will not separate us. We have been so happy.'

THE BOILED EGG

Rosa Macpherson

The boiled egg's face is blank and unseeing, although the eyes are pretty enough. The lashes are long and curled; the green eye-shadow below the arched brows is expertly applied. The black, crayonned hair falls between the eyes, careless, but deliberately so.

The nose, it can be admitted, is drawn haphazardly; mis-shapen and unlifelike.

But it is not the nose, the wrong nose, which makes the eyes blank and unseeing. No, not that.

The mouth is full and red, sensuous even. It wears an expression that is not quite a smile, not at all a frown. It is poised. Yes, poised. For a camera? For an audience? For me?

None of these things matter.

It's the hat. It is the green hat, perched suavely on top of the egg's head, which troubles me. No, it is not the hat, not even the hat, but the slant of the hat. The jaunty slant of the green hat over the eyes. Over the blank unseeing eyes. It is the jaunt; the angle of the hat which torments me so. Which makes my soul weep.

The hat is crayon-green. It is an eggbox hat, torn out and coloured harshly, bluntly. A single strip of sellotape keeps it securely in place, on the smooth hard-boiled head. On the back of the head, so that it does not interfere with the jaunt of the hat.

It does not, even although I know it is there.

The rim of the hat starts just at the edge of the eye, the left eye. It slants upwards towards the right, right over the right eye, then falls, slightly, relaxing above the right ear.

My mother made the hat. My mother made the hat with the angle that is jaunty. My mother, who is not too old, but old enough for me never to have seen her like that. Jaunty. Never to have seen her as poised, as ready, as sure, as expecting, as the boiled egg in the green jaunty hat.

Yet it was my mother who made the hat. It was she who tore the cardboard eggbox at just such an angle so that it would slant; jauntily.

The egg in the green hat makes me sad. It makes me sad for something I do not know.

My mother made the boiled-egg lady for Easter. For my son. At Easter. It is a tradition she has always followed. For me, for my sisters, for my brother, when we were the age of my son.

She does it for him now.

You must take it and roll it and then when the shell is cracked, you must peel off the face and eat what is left.

The priest blessed the egg; you must eat what is left.

My mother gets God into me any way she can.

When I was as young as my son I read Bible stories and when my mother made me a painted boiled-egg head, I would take it and roll it. When the shell was cracked, I would peel off the face and eat what was left.

My son will not do it. My son loves the face and the green hat. He does not want it cracked. So he keeps it, perched on the window-sill, near the television set, and it is still there. Long after Easter.

My mother frowns on this.

She will not understand that things can come in the way of what should be done.

She has always eaten the egg.

Even an egg which has borne such a jaunty hat. Even an egg which has borne such a jaunty hat that she has made.

When she was a young woman and not an old one, she had a son. She called him Mikhaila and she clothed him in girls' dresses. It was all she had. And when the war came and she had to leave her Ukranian home and her Ukranian son, she dressed him in a dress. A pretty white dress, she said, that covered his chubby white knees.

And she walked the length of the dusty road three times before she said goodbye to Mikhaila.

It was a long road, she said.

19

After the war she came back for Mikhaila but Mikhaila was gone. The godless Russians had taken him and he was gone.

Now my mother is an old woman, and when a Russian leader dies, she laughs. My Christian mother laughs because a godless power has died. But her now Russian son is still godless. She left him on the road, and he is godless.

But my son will not eat the egg and she frowns at him.

I let him be, although I too would rather he ate the egg.

The jaunty hat disturbs me and fills all of my head. As long as it is there I can have no life in me, except for the hat. It overbrims my consciousness.

How could my mother make a hat like that and hide her soul so well? Before the hat I knew my mother. Now she is dangerous, a dangerous sighing stranger and when I am with her she makes me breathless. I try to look behind her eyes; behind the layers of aching years and swallowed self.

I cannot see. My eyes are blank and unseeing. They are distorted by my mother's face. I cannot see the Julia for the mother who has nothinged her.

We have eroded the Julia, the jaunty hat-maker, and I would never even have glimpsed her had it not been for the hat. The jaunty angle of the green hat.

My mother once tried to tell me about herself; when she was Julia.

She was in Germany, during the war, and she worked for a farmer. There were four girls altogether. My mother, Julia, was their protector. They feared the farmer but my mother was a giant to him. Anna, she said, was terrified of him. He called them lazy Polish dogs and he would kick them. In the mornings Anna was always up first; ready and terrified. He would kick my mother and the others because they were not as quick as Anna.

Anna slept in her clothes, my mother said, because she was afraid. She did not waste time washing herself, because she was afraid.

My mother, Julia, always undressed herself and she always washed.

My mother, Julia, the giant, took the German farmer to a

people's court and she lifted her torn dress and she showed them her black and bleeding legs. Where he kicked her.

In Germany, during the war, my mother, Julia, took the German farmer to a people's court and she showed them her black and bleeding legs, where he kicked her.

My mother was a giant. Only she was not my mother then. She was Julia.

My mother painted the egg with the blank unseeing eyes.

But it was Julia who made the hat. The green hat with the jaunty slant.

BETTY CORRIGALL

George Mackay Brown

*In the moorland of the island of Hoy in Orkney, right
on the boundary that separates the two parishes of Voes
(Walls) and North Hoy, a gravestone and fence have
recently been erected by some islanders. Underneath lay,
peat-preserved for well over a century, the body of a
young woman who had obviously committed suicide.
Only her name survives: Betty Corrigall. I have let
imagination weave this story about her.*

'No,' said Betty Corrigall, 'I won't go for a walk with you.
Never.'

But at the week's end she walked with the sailor, Willie, as far
as the shore of Moness in North Hoy.

'Kiss you!' said Betty Corrigall. 'What way would I kiss you,
when I don't like you all that much?'

And they walked one evening as far as the sea valley of
Rackwick. A slip of a moon rose over the hill, a silver shaving.
All the Rackwick crofters and fishermen and their folk were
inside. There were sixteen lighted windows, and one dark
window where an old man had died the month before.

At the edge of an oatfield the sailor kissed Betty Corrigall.

'I'll marry you,' said the sailor. 'I'll give up whaling and I'll
build a house for us both. I have enough money to rent a field at
Crockness. There'll be two cows and twenty sheep and a
hundred hens. I'm good with a saw and hammer and nails.
There'll be a bed and a table, three chairs and a deep cupboard.
I'll make a cradle that rocks. A star will shine on the doorstep.'

Betty said she would like that. And he put a storm of kissings
and caressings about her: face and neck and hair.

And Betty Corrigall, she put a dewfall of kisses on his cheek and mouth.

*

Then, about the middle of summer, it happened one morning that Betty Corrigall was sick.

'I think the milk last night was sour,' said her mother.

But in the week that followed, the milk in their porridge at suppertime was sweet and warm from Katie the cow; and every morning Betty was sick.

Her mother put a bitter look on her. Her father said nothing. He went out and looked at the tall green oats beside the house.

'Willie Sinclair, he's wanting to marry me,' said Betty Corrigall. 'He's going to rent a field at Crockness. He'll build a house and make the furniture with his own hands. He's been to the factor to get permission, and to settle about the rent.'

'It's not before time,' said Betty Corrigall's mother. 'He should have made a start months ago. He should be carting the stones now.'

Betty Corrigall's father said it wasn't often a sailor made a good crofter. But still, he had to admit that Willie Sinclair's father had been a hard-working man. 'You could do worse, I suppose,' said her father.

'They've made a bad beginning,' cried Betty Corrigall's mother. 'Let them make sure it doesn't come to a worse end! The way things are, this house is disgraced already. Never till this day did I know my daughter was a slut. The sooner you're out of this house and under that sailor's roof the better it'll be for everybody.'

The father said that if there was no heavy rain, or a gale, between now and August, it would turn out to be a good enough harvest, in his opinion.

Betty Corrigall said that she and Willie Sinclair would have a good life together. She said, so low that her parents could hardly hear her, that she loved him with all her heart.

'The first wooden thing that man had better make,' said Betty's mother, 'is the cradle.'

After the corn began to hang heavy golden heads, Betty did

not put her face out of doors; both because she did not want her ripeness to be seen by the Hoy folk, and also because her mother blackly forbade her – not even to the well for water, not even to drive Katie the cow from the unsickled oats.

But her father secretly left the door unbarred at night, a thing he had never done before.

Night after night, Betty Corrigall and her lover mingled dark whispers, moon-touched whispers, wondering silences.

Yes, Willie the sailor assured her, the factor had agreed to lease him the ten acres for a fair rent. Yes, he had already taken three cart-loads of stone from the quarry to the site of the croft. With great labour, for the place was stony, he had laid a foundation. He had bought enough planks and spars to make the door, window-frames, table, cupboard, bed. ('Make the cradle first,' said Betty Corrigall. 'Make the crib quickly ...') The blacksmith had agreed to make him a plough. He was negotiating with the farmer at the Bu farm about the purchase of a young ox.

And he kissed Betty Corrigall on her cold mouth.

And the darkness took him; and Betty crept inside and barred the door and went into her little lamp-splashed room, until she lost herself soon in the sweet darkness of sleep.

*

Betty's mother waited until her husband went out to the barn. Then she said, 'It will have to be done quietly. I have spoken to the minister. There will be the two witnesses, nobody else. I've made a wide grey coat for you to wear. The marriage is to be in the Manse. I suppose that man's mother – the trollop that she is – will have to be there. And there's to be no drinking or dancing or fiddle-music afterwards.'

Betty Corrigall thanked her mother for having made the arrangements. She herself wanted no more.

And that night Betty Corrigall waited at the gable-end of the croft. The moon was on the wane.

Willie Sinclair did not come that night. Betty had wanted very much to unfold the marriage arrangements to him; also to know what progress was being made with the new croft.

Nor did he come the next night, under the cold ember of the moon.

Betty Corrigall stood there three more nights, and the last night was an utter blackness without stars. The sailor had not come.

*

'Field? A field at Crockness?' said the factor to Tom Corrigall, Betty's father. 'I know nothing about a ten-acre field at Crockness. There is no land at Crockness available. What did you say the young man's name was? William Sinclair. A sailor. I don't know the man. There's a whaling man who's drunk every other night in this ale-house and that. That must be the man. A great teller of tall stories. A great womanizer. So I'm told. Yes, Sinclair's the name – now I remember. Arabella, poor woman, is his mother. I assure you, Tom, even if there was land available, I wouldn't rent a square yard to a fellow like that. No, no, he hasn't carted a single stone from the quarry – never asked – wouldn't get permission if he did ask.'

Betty Corrigall's father, after leaving the factor's office, stood in need of a drink. He dropped in at the ale-house at North Ness. Casually, over drams, he mentioned the name of Willie Sinclair the sailor to Mark the ale-house keeper.

'Gone,' said Mark. 'Cleared out, four days ago. That Yankee ship in Longhope, they signed him on. Bound for Russia. A cargo of grain and clocks. I'm not sorry to see the back of him. He owes me for two bottles of malt – I'll never see that money. I don't grudge it, so he doesn't come back in a hurry. A liar, Tom. A fighter, trouble-maker. Couldn't hold his drink. I hope the bosun of that Yankee ship is a hard man.'

Tom Corrigall drank too many drams of malt that afternoon. Then he went home and struck his daughter hard across the face. A few words blazed like stars in his mouth – sufficient of them to indicate to the appalled woman and the quiet girl how matters stood with regard to Willie Sinclair the sailor, and Betty, and the unborn child, and the house that would be built of wind and sun and rain.

'The door's open,' he shouted to Betty Corrigall at last. 'Go.'

And Betty Corrigall went out into the first silver flakes of winter.

*

Of course the crofter, once he had a good supper of boiled mutton and mashed tatties and neeps in him, was sorry for the things he had done and said, partly out of shock, partly from the fires of whisky he had kindled inside himself; black flames.

He put on his coat, for it was a cold night in early winter, and a few snowflakes drifted like darkling moths athwart the window.

Surely the girl would be at the end of the house, crying perhaps – but quietly, for Betty had never since childhood made wild demonstrations of either grief or joy.

She was not at the gable-end, shawled against the thickening flakeswarm.

She was not in barn or stable or byre, nor over by the well where she loved to linger, listening to the songs of the sweet water deep down, bending to the fugitive gleams and glooms. Betty Corrigall was at no croft or farm in the immediate vicinity. No one had seen her.

The father spent a whole night knocking on angry or blank or anxious doors. He even went to the sailor's mother's house, just at jet-and-russet dawn. 'Here?' said Arabella Sinclair in the cold door. 'No, Betty's not here. I wish she was here. I would have a good daughter at my fire and board. But no, I'm sorry. I haven't seen her for months. Oh yes, that's true enough, *he* left three or four days ago. It's been a quiet house since. I hope you have good word of Betty, and that soon. I love that girl better than the son I bore, and that's the truth.'

Nor was she at the Manse or the factor's or the school-house: places where sapience might have mended the troubles of a breached household.

The man turned for home, after the last door had closed against him.

As his feet slurred through the melting snow, going on the road that skirts the bay at Lyrawa, he saw two fishermen standing at the shore. He knew them; he waved a tired greeting in their direction. The elder fishermen held up his hand, in such a way that it seemed to be a gesture of beseechment and of denial: 'Keep away!' The younger fisherman half turned and then looked down again at a shape in the ebb. His spread hand hung white as a star over it. The body lay face down in a sea-brimmed cleft. But there was no mistaking that spread of golden hair.

*

Oh, it was unthinkable! – a suicide, and a child-burdened suicide at that, to lie among the decent men and women and children in the kirkyard – in God's acre. Neither the kirk session of Voes parish nor the kirk session of Hoy parish would countenance such an intrusion.

A few folk thought it a pitiable business. The girl had gone out of her mind with grief – in such circumstances the word 'suicide' had little meaning. A few others said that, muffled in a snow cloud, she had lost her way and gone over the shallow cliff. And others: she must have gone down to the shore, to see if she could see the American ship dipping between the islands at dawn: and the cold had seized her heart, that was bound to be delicate in her condition; and she had fallen into a rockpool, and was probably dead before the waters closed over her …

It availed nothing, such talk. A hole was dug for Betty Corrigall in the moor, exactly on the border of the two parishes. The gravedigger consulted a map of Hoy with a thin line going across, then sank in his spade again. And there the gravedigger and the father let down the sodden body of Betty Corrigall, with her head in Voes parish and her feet in Hoy parish. Then the gravedigger lit his pipe on the windy moor, and the father opened a whisky flask and passed it to him.

And while that generation of islanders withered slowly into death, one after the other, and after death rotted more urgently until they achieved the cleanness of skeletons, the deep peatmoss kept the body of Betty Corrigall uncorrupted; though stained and darkened with the essences that had preserved it.

Soldiers in the Second World War, digging drains in the moor, came on the body of Betty Corrigall as it lay crosswise with the line of the two parishes. The young men looked with wonderment into a face that had lingered sweet and beautiful from, it seemed, the first springs of time.

MISS DEFT

Erik Coutts

... but later – when I'd matured – I decided she was oh so much more! And how she haunted me! With those fine, doll's eyes and that tailor-model's stillness, she imposed herself so icily, displayed such cool grandeur, such an elegance of low temperature you might say, that all the while I burned in wretchedness.

I'd hang around the canteen merely to steal a glance, though I well knew she never noticed me. Indeed, I recall how I'd shrink back against the racks of Danish pastries or the oozing, plastic tomatoes – shrink back, that is, from the characteristic pale light which opened about her – for she was a cold, *cold* madonna. The abstracted tilt of the head; the brittle hands barely suggestive of a mortal tone; a figure glowing against an unlit candle, some creature descended from a ceramic frieze. And when I felt I might gaze a little, or failing that, dart these tiny peeks – ten to the minute like any novice pianist at his score – I'd diminish further, into enfeeblement now, almost hopelessness, so weighted in a conviction of inadequacy that I'd sneak out the side door.

The pain, I tell you! The vigils! From that herbalist's doorway, I'd draw a feverish bead upon the sad apartment block, staring into the small hours, never daring to venture closer, neither calm nor collected yet so often ringing with hope. Standing there, I'd enfold about her the garrison comforts of those sleeping souls, protecting her through her surely dreamless nights. And oddly, the street would always bear that nostalgic scent of summer dust freshened by a sparse rain. The Deftian scent, I quickly decided, thereafter detecting it whenever I'd think of her. For hours on end, across a hundred nights, and warm as any lunatic, I inhaled that musk! But always – around three in the morning – I'd lose heart just a little. Then the moon would dip. The sky would close. I'd go home.

Then one Derby Day, I received my first promotion. Up steps cheery Mr Occold, his built-up shoe all the while announcing: September ... September. I'd been packing cartons of millet, when he pops his head round the plastic strip curtains and gives me the good news:

'You see, Nigel, that's exactly how we make decisions at Full of Pep: sniff out promise in a youngster. The nose, you know. Always rely on the nose, Nigel. Sniff ... is he likely? ... sniff again ... *more* than likely? ... sniff, sniff, sniff – and then, it's bang up that ladder, yes it is! How long have you been with us now lad?'

'Seven years, Mr Occold,' I reply through excited, trilling sinuses.

'Now you will vindicate my old nose, won't you, lad?'

'Oh, but I will. Yes, yes, I will!'

On the Saturday, I bought a new pair of overalls and a fresh jar of Brylcreem, and on the Monday I ascended the tiled steps to the second floor. There, I counted tins of cat food. Which of course was so much better than canary seed and better by far than those endless and droopy packs of hamster grist – more solid, I suppose, had a better feel to it. And there was the matter of the extra money: seventy pounds per annum plus a higher overtime rate – which latter item counted for so much at F.O.P. because all of us worked like coolies on the Canadian Pacific. You did things at a run and, as it were, over incredible distances. Still, I'd never known any other technique and, from the start, willingly did my share. I even raised my momentum. Output per hour became my religion. With such heavier, more responsive merchandise, my handling and stacking skills became legendary. I made up packs with a ludicrous dexterity. (Even now, I can fill a trolley at Sainsbury's in one minute twenty – fifty seconds flat if it's the last week of the month and I'm living out of tins.)

Actually, promotion was more than opportune, for after seven (could it be *seven*?) years at F.O.P., I'd begun to lapse, even dawdle. My daily average had dropped to forty tonnes, which of course was only twelve over par. It wasn't that I'd lost faith in the company or anything quite so subversive – no, I was simply obsessed. And my productivity had suffered. My mind drifted so easily. My blood just wouldn't cool! My nostrils were rheumy from her perfume. So affected too were my nerves that my hands had started to shake; I could stir the morning tea merely by holding the cup. I had grown edgy. I worried incessantly for her welfare, became fearful even of some pending, though hardly delineated, catastrophe. Perhaps she'd leave? Or die? Or get married, for God's sake? Was she ill? Why hadn't she been there at lunchtime? I fretted. I shook. I searched everywhere for diversions.

Thus, decadence personified, I'd know exactly when the tea whistle was poised to blow, could hear the first chafings of that pea. Close to slouching, indifferent to rindy collars and world affairs, I had stopped grooming my hair. My requirement for salt tablets plummeted. Mrs Brain's energizing grills went untouched, her hair-dos uncomplimented (for the first time actually reminding me of various aquatic plants atop various lifeless ponds). To crown it all, my muscles were losing their tone; if not running soft then surely running scared, all of a sudden unresponsive uncaring things.

When the odd pillar of Courser Number One began to wobble, I could summon the old dynamism only after huge effort, as you might draw a nail from a stubborn rafter. Naturally, at its outset, the condition had worried me, yet no sooner would the anguishing begin than I'd find myself thinking of her – and all tensions would disappear. I'd drift down a gear and, incomparably dimpled in stupidity, my fixed smile would take over. Looking back on that period, I can honestly say I was set fair for decline – a thirty-tonne slob if ever there was one.

Then – Mr Occold: his inference of further advancement, even some future role 'upstairs'. Upstairs! ... Provisioning! Oh, how I whinnied! – because she – correction, *she* – worked on that very floor! Personal Sec. to old Mr Last, who'd perfected the steam-pelleting of dog foods long before I was born. She typed his letters and arranged his diary, tidied his desk and coordinated his antacid programme. If you believed the gossips, he was totally dependent upon her. (I believed those gossips!)

So, there it was: one day I'd elevate to Provisioning. And so bewitching was the prospect that I resolved on a few years of unstinting, intensified labour. Were it to take a billion tins of Cats' Ayes, I'd be ready. I'd work fourteen hours a day, laugh off the chilblains and neglect my tropical fish, have my eyes tested when they failed and re-tested when the re-failed. No task would find me lacking – neither in the forearm nor the small of the back.

And so, my entire being fed upon the heroic lusts of ambition, I buckled down to a vast labour, even disciplining myself to the prospect of Deftless meals (for now I underwent different shifts and ate in the drearier Sir Harry Whittle canteen). How I worked! Engrossed, straining, re-tuned and spiritually lithe, I swept a ream of months before me. Pleasingly too, I also attained fresh levels of fantasy, discovering that from my essentially noble imagery it was possible to draw both solace and stimulus. For hours on end, I'd talk to her. We'd picnic by streams or an accordion-bright Seine, study sunsets or eat Cadbury's Flake. All the while I was swathed in chivalrous intent, but all the while too I built unprecedented tower blocks of Best Friend, clocking up a twelve-point nine hour average and a mite below fifty tonnes. Mr Occold felt I was doing well – 'coming along fine' – but advised me nonetheless to relax, to utilize a full hour for lunch and sundry pleasures, and, most emphatically, to beware hernias. I laughed and in response stock-piled and stock-took five hundred thousand cans by mid week. Then I lifted nineteen hundred four packs by whistle time Saturday. On the Sunday, stooping indelicately for a misplaced packet of daphnia, I herniated.

A second reason I couldn't see her. Yes, I was given a Bic pen and put on light work. Yes, I worked a more civilized shift. But do consider: I was stuffed away in a linseed-glistening cubby-hole and made directly responsible to Miss Litigant – which was unfortunate for anyone, heroes included. I drew graphs and I pinned them up. I made lists and stored them away.

Furtively, I memorized Spanish verbs. I watched the downward drift of tiny spots before my eyes. I was utterly trapped. Time swam upon a gravy sea. Beyond the chimneys, the clouds merged as always into the face of a labrador, with a pair of asymmetric eyes and a muzzle flecked in the high soot ...

Then Mr Last was found dead in his greenhouse. Had a stroke, they said. The flag came down. The factory closed for a day. We subscribed towards a colossal wreath and stood in the withering tail of a rainbow and listened to the words and watched him put away. He'd never spoken to me and I knew him only as the white hair in the Daimler. There wasn't therefore a personalized flavour to my thoughts during that funeral (other than the normal selfish one, I mean), but I recognized only too well that things would change after this, for amongst the consequences of any departure that's the frontrunner.

And change they did: I was promoted. Again. Out of the blue, as before. Yet now, my elation was tempered, almost dampened, by feelings of unease and inadequacy, for it transpired that I was to be nothing less than Personal Ass. to Alex Astrolobe. They'd given him Provisioning. In a way, I was flattered ... Astrolobe! ... the company whizzkid who'd proved that while the same strict palatability constraints may fool a dog, a hamster or a tortoise, they never would a cat, a rat or a terrapin; the same Astrolobe who, from the stringy peril of his Tiger Moth, had dropped one thousand shortbread voles* on Scunthorpe during that big launch. Such were the stories of this careerist that for days I was gripped by overemphatic giddiness, up to that very moment indeed when I knocked on the fresh-gilded door. And how those panels swam! – at divergent angles, they formed a perfect vortex, and I felt closer to an end than a beginning, almost forced as I was to uncontrolled hammering, but snapping to at the moment the Balliol voice bade me enter – which I did, following the echo through the smoke and up to the squat torso at the A-shaped desk.

'Ah, Stukely!' he said, his forehead drawing up into a dozen challenging runnels. 'You're acroase there. Got a pen?'

* Contained within shatterproof plastic, of course.

I produced Miss Litigant's ballpoint. He pointed towards a mountain of paper.

'Then straight to it, Stukely! That's how it's done in my set-up – how many hours can you manage?'

He flopped into his velour chair and unashamedly scratched his velour legs. From his thrusting chin I could observe the radiance of a few (very minor) sparks.

'Twelve?' I suggested in a whisper.

'Not on, laddie! Sorry – not here. Fourteen's nearer my standard.'

'That would suit me ... really very well, Mr Astro–'

One of his four telephones buzzed restfully. And, making furious notes, he spoke into its snout for two hours. When he rang off, he looked at me vacantly. All the lustre had drained from his yellow eyes.

'Oh yes – Stukely. Well, how's it going?'

'Oh, I'm just fine, thank you.'

'I meant the work.'

'But you never ... uh, you never really told me what to do. If you remember, I showed you my pen and –'

'Oh my God, they've sent me a moron! Now look: if I've got to show you everything, you're simply no good to me. But, I'll make it clear just this once ... pen?' (he pointed) ... 'paper?' (he pointed) ... 'desk?' (he was still pointing) ... 'then get on with it!'

Gosh, I sat so miserably by that pile, making groping little ticks in random corners, grateful even for the cramp in my forefinger, for at least that asserted some sort of independence. At eleven, I brought his coffee. Astrolobe was incredibly hunched, talking like a machine pistol into three telephones, pop-eyed, knotty-veined. Whilst the pen in his right hand added five columns of figures, that in his left pursued its own blazing shorthand.

'Stukely, don't hang about – pour it into me!'

I poured it into him, all the while looking into the yellow eyes.

'Yes ... no ... top offer ... yes, yes, quite ... glug ... hah! ... you're joking! ... for salted rusks ... glug, glug ... no comment ...'

34

By midday I'd ticked my way through a hog's weight in counterfoils, though Astrolobe was only forty minutes advanced in dictation. My head was well down, and I was feeling pretty wretched I'll say, filled with that special languor which overtakes the low in spirit. I'd started a fresh series of concentric rings but, suddenly, so keenly conscious of apathy and guilt, I felt close to being physically sick. My pen couldn't manage another revolution. How I craved the odd tonne of crates! Clammy, utterly wearied from inactivity, and quite griped about the haunches, I spun round in my chair:

'Mr Ast–'

I gasped. Began to shake. Throat ... throat went dry. Couldn't say a word, because there – over there – *she* was seated by his desk, and revered in a cold lace, her copper mane beguiling the sunlight. Her pen flew over the notepad. And as she took down the drivel, her expression maintained that same sublime disdain which I'd often marvelled at, if hitherto from only the very farthest reaches. She was staring at the ceiling.

'Yes, yes, Stukely – what is it?'

'I ... I wondered – '

'Wrong!' he snarled, his face going about its conflicting routes like putty applied in anger. 'Just never do that, Stukely! We uphold effort in this department, not wonder. Fetch some coffee!'

In misery, I departed, fetched the coffee and made to pour the scalding liquid into him (well trained, eager to please).

'Stukely! What – the hell – are you – doing?'

'I thought – '

'Look, here's some fresh material. Just leave all the thinking to me!'

So fiercely did I redden that my hairline started to singe. Although she had repositioned her glass hands, Miss Deft had taken not the slightest interest in the little scene and maintained her scrutiny of the ceiling. I slunk to my corner.

*

Through the coming weeks I doodled in the acutest misery. I longed for something meaningful in the work, were it only a barrage of complaints from the suppliers who received my stuff. But nothing, nothing whatsoever. Astrolobe created even greater quantities of paper. His life appeared to draw its sustenance from paper, feeding upon it in the same way a plant will use the sun. It appeared he maintained copies of everything – his 'brought forwards', a series of cross-checks intended to provide surveillance upon the universe in general and trade enemies in particular – arranging and rearranging all the while, even through the drama of his telephone marathons, so coiling the cables they'd eventually unleash like catapults and almost strangle him. At times I grew so bemused by it all I forgot to become demoralized.

My only pleasure lay in counting the minutes to eleven a.m., for then of course *she* would apear, like some precisely crafted clockwork bird at the stroke of the first chime. And when I'd hear those indifferent, brittle steps approach, or perhaps distinguish some cold variant within the perfume behind me, I'd positively peal with happiness! Every cloud would lift. I'd breathe deeply, share that air. By a few, intensely wrought currents, I would deliver ardent and poetic declarations – rearwards, naturally – into that lovely, Deftian ether. I'd compel my shoulders to an incredible expansion, make them shoulders anyone should notice. And, had she known how to de-code messages delivered by an end-elevated view of my wriggling ears, I should have begun an immediate transmission. During those hours, my emotions ran the fullest spectrum, from major to minor indeed, from hope to resignation. And by the time she completed her duties, when those departing steps announced April ... April, I was consumed in romantic despair.

But! Oh yes – but! A development: Astrolobe grew charming, became altogether greased in charm. At dictation, his voice was now felicitous, clarinetish. It smiled through its registers. Perceptibly, his pace slowed or, rather, modulated. He also laughed a great deal. The room reeked of gallantry. I could picture his eyes odiously lightening all the while, pools where lizards played!

Excessive courtesies flowed; small caring pauses; ever more considered and courtly verbiage streaming forth to a hundred traders in breadcrumbs, cuttlefish and ox hearts. At five to eleven, he would race to the executive washroom, returning in Bruted smugness and flashing vulgar college cufflinks. He'd cancel his calls, straighten his tie, flatten that single, skullsplitting weft, fidget, pace, fidget, cough his cough and, finally, full of those back-of-the-throat chortles Oxford men manage so well, he would escort her to her chair ...

He even fetched the coffee. And when he was gone, her presence would agitate my poor system further, my face exploring fresh ranges of red, my lower bowel watchful and controlled. I ticked like mad. My ears sang their sad melodies. My shoulders would grow into barn doors. And on *his* return, I'd quietly command: 'Don't mess about, man – just pour it into me – can't hang about here, got thousands of ticks to make – dammit, you idiot! – spilled all over the requisitions – oh my God, a moron! ...' But he never heard. Actually, he didn't bring me a coffee at all. He just sat there on the axis of the A and made revolting cosseting sounds, likely taking in his coffee with the fastidious, unhurried elegance of some insect on a trove of pollen. Sometimes, he even cooed. Imagine! To *my* beloved!

I guessed he discerned my feelings towards her, for he chose a particular beastly technique in order to belittle me:

'Memo to Nigel Stukely: Please note that lunch hour means precisely what it say, dash, one hour and no longer, capital enn, capital ell. Take heed, Stukely – I shall not be inclined to overlook bad, capital bee – Bad – timekeeping within my Department. Accordingly, you are warned that this practice shall cease forthwith, capital cee, capital eff, Miss Dee ...'

'Memo to Nigel Stukely: It has come to my attention that twenty tonnes of Wet Nose extrusions (value £25,000) have been disposed of as pig swill, and that Consignment Note 5050 provided authorization for this incredible transaction. Investigate forthwith – provide proof of your exemption from blame – and report to me as a matter of the utmost urgency, capital yoos, there's a pet ...'

Pet! It was pet now, was it? I writhed! My right eyeball pursued unilateral objectives. My hand shook. I clenched the Bic. It snapped. Wail went my soul, oozeglob went the Bic. My hand shook in blue oil. My mind careered into vivid, orange glens. Oh Great God of Jealousy! Heaving in fury, I forged his name across many forms. My pen grew balletic. Soon I had compiled a tidy shopping list, including thousands of tonnes of rusks (capital arr, Goddammit), miles of steel cable, countless A-shaped desks, a truss of Range Rovers, two villas in Biarritz and the prize camellia at Kew.

For weeks, I purchased diverse treasures (my personal favourite, that fine early Reynolds of Squire Thrift). But for weeks, too, I absorbed threats and chastisement through the medium of memoranda. I grew obese from insults. Still, it was clear that no other name as often entered my *liebchen*'s mind, and I found that heartening. But did it enter her *thoughts*? I wondered, as I put the finishing touches to the Bream Valley Zoo project. Did she ever once consider that faceless sufferer – as other than the instigator of epic bungles, I mean? I feared not.

Nonetheless, Astrolobe fared no better, for she treated him with complete indifference, that reflection in my tobacco tin never once relinquishing its utter, waxwork immobility. And in the small hours, I'd smile at the thought. I had returned to the herbalist's doorway, there imbued with fatalism, though sometimes too a fierce, nihilist's joy which fortified my darkness. Now, the nights were unscented and bleak. It was lonely as ever. Yet, one grim evening, I was disconcerted to observe the figure of a man lurking in the shadows opposite. And, for as long as I remained there, so did this fellow, never moving, merely facing me in silhouette or, sometimes, within the penumbra of a quickdrawn cigarette. Clearly, this provided an eerie few hours. When I departed I was inclined to more than one backward glance, I'll say. And yet, I did not expect a repetition that following night, but there again he was, drawn back in the shadow. Now, I felt distinctly uneasy. Perhaps he was a policeman? Checking out this regular loiterer?

Yes, that seemed likely. And now, unease gave way to outright worry, for, though willing to be classified in many ways, in that solitary pastime of mine I resented any ignoble implication. (Me? Nigel Stukely?) The very thought made me blush!

Still, on the third night I had remembered to strew my person with symbols of innocence and highmindedness – a book of sonnets, a collection of pressed flowers, Goodall's *Freshwater Fishes*, a portrait of the Queen, that sort of thing – and as I studied the figure of my companion, I snorted with self-righteousness. However, he did not venture towards me, neither then nor during the nights which followed.

My nerves were in a bad state. Eventually, I couldn't bear the situation and I resolved to challenge him. But at the very moment I advanced into the street, I found Miss Deft herself bearing down upon me along the nearside pavement! For the merest corner of a second, I suspected some form of divine intervention, but at the sight of her glassy gaze, I quelled into a red confusion, making to run. Then, he opposite – my nightly companion – crossed the street at a run, intercepting Miss Deft, but facing me.

'Astrolobe!' I gasped.

'Correction, Stukely: Mister Astrolobe.'

Something went snap.

'Look here, Astrolobe – look here, you creep, what are you doing? ... what are you playing at?'

He took Miss Deft's hand in his.

'Allow me to escort you home, my dear,' he said in his courtly, ochre-coloured way.

For her part, she gazed at the bowls of frondy buck-you-ups, or the dried bananas perhaps.

'Look here, Astrolobe – don't you ever call that – that – angel of a woman "my dear"! Why, you're not fit to breathe the same air!'

At once, his brow unrolled. His mouth splayed. Then his eyes swelled in horror as though he'd only that minute arisen from a fall in a doggy glade. In the grim silence, we glared at one another. Then he laughed:

'You ghastly oik!' he said through bared teeth.

'Ghastly oik yourself!' I shouted.

'Memo to Nigel Stukely: With immediate effect, your employment within the Full of Pep Group is terminated. Not going too fast for you – my dear?'

But she didn't reply. She was counting the Artex spikelets within the shop.

'Oh come away with me, Miss Deft!' I wailed, clutching her Dorothy bag to my breast. 'I just can't bear you being at the mercy of ... this creep! ... this careerist! Just look at his eyes!'

'You Council House pup!' yelled Astrolobe, grabbing at my shoulder.

'Don't ... you ... *lay hands* on me, Astrolobe!'

We tussled: he gouged my eye. I smote him with the Dorothy bag. When we withdrew to opposite corners, tousled and gasping, we realized she had gone.

'Miss Deft! Come back!' I cried, running after the sounds of her crisp heels and fighting Astrolobe all the while.

*

Only later did we learn the full extent of poor Miss Deft's injuries on that staircase.

Now we push her in the park, taking turns. Alex swings his stick. Sometimes, he takes his dog. We're all friends now. I stare at the back of her fine head. What she is thinking, goodness only knows, for, other than an occasional, yearning, notional loneliness about the eyes, she never lets on. She gets cold a lot.

VLAMERTINGE

Lorn Macintyre

Her hands swam up the dim mirror; the same rope-trick of hair done for sixty years to the pipe of the same blackbird, it seemed. One hand compressed the coil; the other rummaged the fluted dish for grips.

All the time the mouth seemed to be mocking itself.

Next, a hat, from the dozens stacked inside each other in the precarious cardboard boxes around her. That was one good thing about being old; your clothes stopped dating.

Now the hands were fitting on a grey felt helmet. She had to sit on the edge of the bed, using a piece of horn to lever somebody else's shoes over the latticed stockings. She dressed herself at jumble sales.

A dab of powder paled her cheeks before she snapped shut the handbag. She put her fare inside her glove, then tried the door with her knee.

Apart from the milk and mail vans, she was the only traffic now on the avenue, the laird so long dead she would have to work out the date. Wheels pulled by hooves had brought two kings, the foreign one asking for seconds of her grouse in aspic.

She could have gone up to the village, but she went the other way at Wade's Bridge. It was better to keep the big house bus stop going. She was always in plenty of time. There were things to look at, a tree to move under when it rained.

She put out her hand for the blue bus, but still couldn't get used to dropping the exact coins into the perspex slot, seeing the ticket spat out. Other old ones had passes in plastic wallets that got them on for nothing; she didn't like that, and could manage on what she had.

In the old days the conductress would have sat down beside her, giving her news. Now the bus seemed so big, all the heads hidden by the high seats.

She clarified the window with a glove, but it was going too fast. Anyway, they couldn't stop building; such ugly houses. The town was a small city now. Horses hadn't needed horns. Now they would take the legs off you, and say they hadn't seen you.

'Next!'

She tried to wait in the post office queue, but an elbow dunted her back. She had to go to the strange face behind the screen.

'You could save yourself a journey,' he advised, tearing the leaf from the book. 'This can be cashed at Invernevis.'

Maggie nodded and smiled. She preferred to take the bus five miles every Thursday, rather than let that bitch Chrissie MacSween see her business. Besides, it was somewhere to come.

The man shrugged off the vagaries of the pensionable, his stamp thumping before he dealt out.

She took her notes to the shelf, beside the chained pen, opened her handbag and did some counting with somebody else's tortoiseshell spectacles.

The bank was just along the street. People touched her arm, but there wasn't time today to stand aside and talk about the old days; though she stopped to see who it was this time on the black-bordered card in the butcher's window.

She put the ten pounds inside her savings book in the trough with the envelope, her private pension from the late laird's lawyers. You had to be careful you didn't get your hand caught in the trough. For robbers, apparently; toughened glass between people now.

'How are you today, Mrs Macdonald?' the nice young fellow asked.

She'd tried to slip him a pound for himself at Christmas, but he'd pushed it back, explaining that they weren't allowed to take money. The next time she'd put a packet of cigarettes (gold ones) in the trough; they hadn't come back.

'How much have I got now?'

He was surprised by the question. 'I'll have to go and work it out.'

When he came back with her book he put both hands into the trough, pointing out the total with his pen. She had to get out the spectacles.

'As much as that?'

'It mounts up, with the interest.'

'And if I wanted to take it all out, would that be all right?'

'You don't mean *in cash*, Mrs Macdonald?'

They had one old man who came in at the busiest time on the last day of the month. He drew out all his savings, stacked the small notes in a suitcase, then sat for the afternoon at a table, counting it out before paying it back in. Of course it had to be checked again by the teller.

'I might mean that,' Maggie said. 'I'll be back later.'

She wasn't studying the plastered offers to faraway places on the window: she was peering, trying to see what the faces were like beyond.

The white plastic chair was very uncomfortable. The young woman in the blue blazer had a thing like a television set beside her.

'Where do you want to go?'

Maybe it was the made-up eyes on her headgear that put Maggie off.

'I'm not sure.'

'Not sure?' It was said as a rebuke. 'Pensioners only get the cheap rate in Spain in the winter.'

'It's not Spain,' Maggie said.

Painted nails were now drumming the desk.

'Italy? Is that it? You won't see the Pope in Rome in the summer.'

'I don't want to go to Italy,' Maggie told her.

'Look: go and decide.' (She was leaning over the desk now.) 'Then come back and we'll see what we can do' – a way of saying *I don't want to see you again.*

'If I get abroad, what will I need?' Maggie asked.

The tailored shoulders shrugged. 'It depends where it is. You may need an injection.'

43

'An injection?' Maggie echoed, alarmed. Once was enough; at the old laird's insistence, after she'd stood on a rusty nail.

'And of course a passport, which you can get through the post office, depending on your destination, which we don't know yet, do we?' Her eyes were taking it out on Maggie's hat. 'There's somebody waiting.'

Back to the post office, where a form was pushed under the shield.

'Two small photos, signed on the back by someone who can vouch for you,' the man explained. 'You'll get them at the station.' His eyes said: *gaga*.

She found the booth in the corner, by the left-luggage lockers. The girl behind the bookstall gave her some ten pences, but with no grace.

She tugged the curtain behind her. The directions required close scrutiny with the tortoiseshells as she sat on the basic stool. *Select decorative background you require.* She turned, to a choice of bare wall or a scrap of blue curtain. She left it. *Adjust seat to reflect desired image position in glass.* Her shoes pushed, and she was facing the other way.

She stood, her backside out of the curtain, twisting the damn thing, but when she sat down again she was still too wee for the frame. She tried again, the other way, and was too tall till another twist brought her down. There was far too much of her hat, but it would have to do.

Insert coins when green light is on. It was on now. A ten pence fell; that took some finding.

She sat, staring at the green light in the dark depth behind the reflecting glass, her hands up on her hat. The flash took her by surprise. She was bending to get her glove when the second flash came.

She jerked up and just saw the green light going before she was blinded.

She was tidying the small scarf at her throat when the last chance came.

That wasn't very successful, she thought as she got herself out. *Photos delivered here*, an arrow pointed down. Then a girl came along, jingling money in her fist to the tune from the red transistor she was swinging in her other hand. Her legs jived as if about to go from under her. Her hair was bright yellow, like flames.

'It's being used,' Maggie told her.

But her voice went for nothing in the racket. The girl shrugged and stepped through the curtain. Maggie saw the transistor set down by the floppy green footwear.

She stood with her ear to the machine. She didn't know how it worked, but it couldn't do both of them together. In the last flash from the short curtain she had an image: her hat imposed on that yellow mess.

That was both their money wasted. The silly girl; why were the young always in such a hurry?

The girl emerged with a new tune to move to. They both hung about. Maggie looked around, then gave the machine an elbow, to see if it would yield up her money. She was watching a woman she thought she knew at the bookstall when the girl pulled her arm and pointed.

She had come out of the slot head first. She picked them up by the corner. She wasn't going to let that cheeky girl see. Anyway, she needed her spectacles, so she went into the empty waiting-room – a fire that looked as if it hadn't been lit for years.

She sat and studied herself through tortoiseshell in black and white. Now what use were two views of her hat? In the next one, she looked as if she wasn't all there. The last one would have to do, though her eyes and mouth were wide open.

Then she remembered that the man had said two. But she wasn't going to go through all that palaver again, though the girl was swaying away from the booth, studying a strip of herself.

She slumped in the waiting-room, very disappointed. Usually she went to see her friend Mrs Thomson, who ran a sweet shop. She brought round her own chair for Maggie so that they could chat as she served, Maggie nibbling away at a dark choc ice which she insisted on paying for, because Mrs Thomson had to keep her stock right for the Italian.

But she wasn't in the mood today; nor to look round the shops. She wasn't going to be able to manage this business

45

herself. It wasn't just the difficult questions on the form, and the photographs; she didn't know where she was going.

*

She got off the bus in the village, where she rarely went. All the old ones were wanting to stop her and speak about how things had changed for the worse since the old laird, with the trustees pushing up the rents.

But she wasn't going to stop because they'd said plenty about the old laird behind his back; plenty about her too, in days when she needed friends. She had learnt the hard way; it was best to keep to yourself.

She went up the lane and opened wrought-iron, gravel making her shoes unstable. Her gloved fingers slipped round the rhododendron bloom, lifting it to her face as if it was a wine whose bouquet she had to pronounce on.

The bell jangled at the back of the house, and a shadow came towards the stained glass.

'Mrs Macdonald! My, but it's nice to see you!'

The housekeeper meant it. She regarded the small woman in the elfin hat on the step as being superior to all those in the village, not only because she'd been the old laird's confidante as well as his housekeeper: there was a dignity here that hadn't rubbed off.

Maggie followed Miss Grant through the old-fashioned hall; burnished brass; a black hat hanging by a mirror.

'Father MacInnes is in the garden, with the bees.'

'I don't want to disturb him,' Maggie said hastily.

'He'll be very pleased to see you.'

She sat on the edge of the floral sofa till he came in.

'The bees are a bit restless,' he explained, shaking hands. 'That's a sign of thunder.'

She nodded. He had kept hives on the big house lawn in the old days. Visored and gloved, he had presented her with the first comb of the season. Father MacInnes had been one of the old laird's closest friends, sitting up with him late into the night over the habitual decanter, his worries about the estate treated as confession.

46

There was mutual admiration. This little fresh-faced woman in the neat hat had been so good to the old laird, asking nothing but that he was happy. The priest sat close, turned to her on the sofa.

'You're looking well, Maggie.'

'Oh yes, Sir,' she said earnestly.

He was too experienced to know that this wasn't a rare social call. People liked to come round in their own good time.

'How is Iain?'

Her son was one of the most successful QCs at the Edinburgh Bar. That was one piece of big house business she was glad everyone knew: it was the old laird's money that had put the boy through school and university, though he'd made his own way after that.

Iain had tried hard to make her give up her cottage and go through to Edinburgh with him, to his fine house in the New Town. But who else would put flowers on the graves of those she'd served and loved all these years? It wasn't something that clever words could explain. But one sadness was that Iain hadn't married. Too busy courting the law, he said.

'He'll be made a judge soon,' Father MacInnes assured his mother.

Miss Grant brought in the tray, spreading the napkin for her, setting down blue china near her, leaving the priest to pour.

'I'll see you before you go, Mrs Macdonald,' the housekeeper said before closing the door behind her with that discretion that knew that difficult things were said in that room.

Father MacInnes held out a plate. It wasn't because she could see that the scones would be inferior to her own that made Maggie refuse. She needed her mouth for other things. But she was glad of the tea, and took an extra lump with the clawed tongs.

'There's something you want to say to me, isn't there?' the priest said, taking a scone.

'It's *Miss* Macdonald.'

He nodded. Like everyone else in the village, he assumed that her boy belonged to the old laird, though there had never been a confession.

'And I'm eighty today.'

'I would never believe it,' he said, shaking his head in true wonder. 'Many happy returns, Maggie; you'd better have a bit of Miss Grant's cake.'

She only took it after he'd halved the slice.

'So I said to myself: it's got to be done now.'

He listened, eating cake himself to relax her.

'If it would make you feel any better, we could go through to the wee chapel I've got here.'

She shook her head. She'd rather say it to his face than to a screen.

'This was all in the time of Father Macdonald – and he didn't know?'

'No, Sir.' She could have added that his predecessor had never been liked down at the big house.

Telling about it after such a long silence brought it all back, and she cried. He put his arm round her shoulders, but she had to get it out, though it was choking her.

'And Iain knows?'

She looked at him, aghast. 'Oh no, Sir. He *mustn't* know.'

He was surprised by this. 'But it's nothing to be ashamed about. Lawyers like the truth.'

'We've never talked about it, Sir. I suppose he believes what the rest believe. That's the way I want to leave it.'

'There's very little to go on,' he said after a silence in which she had a little bunch of lace up to her face.

'If I only knew, one way or the other, it would make such a difference.'

The priest's hands were clasped between his knees as if the pattern of the carpet contained the solution.

'Tell me, Maggie: why now, when you've managed so long?' It was said compassionately.

'Because it's my birthday, Sir. You can't go on forever.'

He nodded, having nothing in his faith to contradict her. Now he was rubbing his chin, as if testing his morning shave.

'Well now; there are *some* details; perhaps I'd better write them down. Come into my study.'

Now she was sitting at his desk. He was writing what she was saying, his spectacles on. She watched the careful gold nib.

'It so happens that I'm interested in this kind of thing,' he said, looking at her over his frames.

She had remembered the old laird lending him books, and had heard them talking. That was why she had come.

'I'll write tonight, Maggie.'

Both hands were in her bag, bringing out the passport form and strip of photos.

'It's a bit early; you hold on to them till I see what I can find out.'

But she was passing him her bank savings book.

'I've got the money, Sir.'

Iain used to send her big cheques, but she'd posted them back, and they'd stopped coming.

He pushed the book back without opening it. 'You keep that too, Maggie, till we see what happens. Now I think we should say a little prayer.'

The felt hat went down over the clasped handbag.

*

Sundays excepted, the dawn train to the south came up the gradient above her cottage, through her bedsprings, climbing her old bones; no better alarm.

But the bed was empty, its springs a muffled harp. She had been up for most of the night, taking down boxes, easing drawers, hats lifted into, removed from the mirror: this one too bold; the feather on the next sad-looking. Jumpers from jumbles were held up in front of her: not nice at the neck.

By the time the blackbird was singing, she was dressed from head to foot, the little case on the bed having clothes folded into it; trying to guess a climate; erring on the side of warmth.

Talcum, a pair of scissors, a skein of stockings. The case was crammed; she had to sit on it. Breakfast was a little brown pot of tea, two aspirins, her habit of getting through the day since the old laird's death.

She had her gloves on at seven when the horn sounded. A final check to make sure the cooker switch was up. She looked around, as if there was some doubt that she would be seeing that kitchen again. The door handle got a good shake as Father MacInnes, casually dressed, put her case into his boot.

'Well, Maggie, are you ready for the big adventure?'

There was a moment of fear as they turned out of the avenue, but the mountains closed in for the way south. Sometimes they talked, and sometimes she looked out of the window, all that heather reminding her of all those grouse she'd plucked, having to be hung till the meat was moving. She couldn't have stomached it herself.

Father MacInnes was a very careful driver, especially on the bends. But when they got on the motorway, lorries crashed by. The wayside crows seemed unconcerned. They had a first stop for petrol. It had already been decided that they were going to share the expenses, though Maggie had wanted to pay everything.

'I was going to take a summer holiday anyway,' he said, and took charge of the money and the papers.

They stopped at a Little Chef for coffee. Maggie was shocked at the sizzling hamburgers being flipped on the griddle. Fancy cooking directly on top of the stove.

Now the sinking sun was flaring the windscreen, and though the priest pulled down the visor on her side, she nodded off like a baby in the harness of the seat belt. She was travelling, lurching in a gig, up the rutted avenue to the big house, clutching the arm of the driver as the sunlight through the filter of trees rippled dark flames along the horses' backs.

'This is our stop for the night,' Father MacInnes was telling her.

It had been an old coaching inn, the interior modernized. A lift took Maggie up to her reservation. It was a mistake; it should only be a single room.

'It's let as a single,' the receptionist told her, opening another door. 'This is the bathroom.'

Maggie was alarmed at the thought of it opening into her bedroom, till the waitress explained that it was hers only.

'All our rooms have private facilities.'

It looked very expensive, but she trusted Father MacInnes. When the girl left her with the key she sat on the edge of the bath, steeping her feet, wishing she had some salt. She was standing in the shallows of the evening loch, squirming her toes into the warm sand. There was another pair of feet, bigger, the toes bunched by cast-off boots. He was holding her hand.

'Will you do something for me?' he asked.

She was frightened. She turned her face to the hill where the sun was going down, behind the standing stones. She had trusted him. Her ankles felt as if they were being clasped by icy hands.

'Will you let down your hair?'

It made her laugh out, across the loch.

'Some time,' she promised, not letting go of his hand.

It was Father MacInnes knocking; she had to dry her feet quickly.

They went down to the dining-room; dark wood, scarlet seats. The cutlery was King's Pattern; nothing like what they'd had at home in the silver safe.

The seating was in facing benches, like sitting on a gig. Maggie had to put on her tortoiseshells to read the menu. Everything was so expensive. Usually she bought a wee bit of fish, or some bacon, to fry in home farm butter. When you'd cooked all these courses for somebody else all your life, you couldn't be bothered for yourself.

'I'll have the hamburger,' she told the waitress.

Father MacInnes raised his eyebrows.

'Try anything once,' Maggie said.

He wanted a well-done steak.

'And some wine.' It was Maggie who said it.

'I'll bring the list,' the waitress said.

The tortoiseshells scanned the padded black folder. It was fancy writing, but she could read the prices all right. The old laird had kept a good cellar, mostly for himself. She'd had a set of keys, and had let bottles breathe for royalty.

'Beaune,' she said firmly, closing the book, her good try at French.

'Bottle or half?'

'A half bottle will do,' Maggie said. She didn't want to insult Father MacInnes.

When her plate came, it was an ashet, with a ragged salad. French fries meant a heap of sorry chips.

'Take some of this stuff away,' she told the waitress. In her kitchen waste had been a sin.

'Just leave what you don't want,' the girl said dismissively.

'No,' Maggie said, through a long experience of dealing with difficult maids. She waited till another plate was brought.

The wine came. She had half a glass, but the priest found no difficulty finishing the bottle. Her hamburger looked as if it had been set on fire.

They talked about old times at Invernevis; mostly about the gentleman she'd served. Though the little wine was making her light-headed, she watched her tongue.

He brought the conversation round to what was ahead of them tomorrow.

'You might find it upsetting.'

He wasn't going to tell her what he'd discovered. She was glad of that, otherwise she might have asked him to turn back.

'I'll be all right, Sir,' she said, leaving the rest of the tart. All the goodness had been boiled out of the apples.

She said her prayers before she climbed into the big bed, controls on either side for radio and clock; the snooze-button. Even if she'd been able to understand them, she wouldn't have bothered with them.

She knew she wasn't going to sleep, despite the wine. It wasn't excitement; she was frightened about what she was going to find out tomorrow. She shouldn't have come; she could take a stroke. She'd wanted to go quietly, in her own cottage, with the key turned.

But she knew she had to know. It wasn't only for her peace of mind. That wild threat shouted through the train window that terrible night was because of her. It made her want to sleep. Now she was running down a platform, after a train always out of reach.

She was up in the dawn, her hands in the strange mirror, doing her hair a special way, the felt helmet fitted carefully, like a warrior going to a contest. She gave her nose a final pat with the powder-puff.

She didn't like the look of the boat Father MacInnes drove her into. She made for a window, away from the rowdy school party, but she seemed to shrink into the seat, just managing to see light.

When the hovercraft lifted, the window was pelted with spray, her stomach left behind at Dover. She shut her eyes and thought of that other crossing, by slow boat, black smoke from its tall funnel.

Father MacInnes leaned over. 'I'm going to the Duty Free. Would you like something?'

He had to explain what Duty Free meant. Every Thursday she bought a quarter bottle of whisky in town. A wee drop made her sleep. She asked the priest for a miniature of brandy for her handbag, just in case.

Poplars fell back on either side of the straight roads. Now she was missing hills. She thought of tramping boots, postcards in her bottom drawer. Nothing seemed to have changed.

They stopped at a café. Maggie kept her eye on the alsatian sprawled on the tiles. They'd had a cupboard of gold-rimmed coffee cups in the big house, but never as small as this one. The fat woman seemed to understand what Father MacInnes was saying to her, but Maggie didn't want to bother him for milk, so she gulped the black bitterness; grounds.

'We're in Belgium now, Maggie.'

The countryside didn't look any different, except for the queer crops on poles. Hops, the priest explained. She was getting more and more nervous, wishing she could have a wee drop from the bottle in the handbag on her lap. But if she asked for a stop, she might not be able to go on.

Signposts with names she could never pronounce; someone casting into a canal; red-tiled buildings just as tumbledown as the home farm. Surely they didn't need all these churches.

'Not long now,' the priest promised.

She was praying: *Please let it be all right. As long as I know.*

The car turned off the motorway, bumping to rest on the verge by a few houses.

'Vlamertinge,' Father MacInnes said. 'There are three of them here.' He had a map spread over the steering-wheel, and

53

was looking at his own writing propped against the windscreen. 'We want number two.' He turned to her. 'Do you feel prepared?'

Her hands were on her hat as she nodded. He came round to open the door for her, taking her on his arm as the old laird had always done with lady callers.

The road was narrow, dusty. Wheat almost submerged the low rubble wall, three poplars at the other end. They went down the mowed path. She was a bit unsteady.

He swung the black gate for her. Then he opened what looked like a little safe in the wall and took out a book. He said a row, a number. She could see what kind of place it was now.

'I don't think I want to go any further, Sir,' she said faintly.

'You've come too far, Maggie.'

A young couple had been lying on the turf in the warmth of the evening sun. He buttoned his shirt as they got up, nodding respectfully as they went out.

'It's a beautiful place,' Father MacInnes said as he took her arm along the white rows. He was counting. 'Here you are.'

She was standing at the stone.

SAMUEL RAEBURN
GORDON HIGHLANDERS
Died 3.8.17
Aged 24

He'd come to Invernevis as a groom before the war. He was such a nice, big friendly fellow, always praising her cooking, though God knows, it was nothing fancy that went through to the servants' hall. He spent hours talking to the horses.

As soon as war broke out the local Territorials had gone off, including her own brother Hector; but Sam had stayed. The laird needed the horses to get about, but some of the wives didn't see it that way, and shouted after Sam when he was up alone with the gig in the village. It was in Gaelic, but he knew.

'I'm not going to join up,' he kept telling her as they sat in her kitchen, drinking nothing stronger than tea. But the laird came through with a good shot in him as usual. He seemed irritated to find his groom in the kitchen with Maggie, and kept his eyes on her, making her feel very uncomfortable as he spoke. One night he said: 'If I were you, Raeburn, I'd join up before they bring in conscription.'

'What's that, Sir?' he asked.

'It means making you go.'

'But they couldn't do that, Sir,' Maggie said, shocked.

'With the losses they're having, they'll have to do something. I would go myself, if it wasn't for this damn leg.' He slapped his right thigh, the limb permanently straightened by shrapnel in South Africa. 'Think about it, Raeburn,' was the last thing he said before going back through to his decanter.

They sat in silence in the fading light.

'He's calling me a coward,' Sam said eventually.

'He's not; he's just had too much,' she reassured him, putting her hand over his.

'I'll show him,' he vowed.

'You'll do nothing of the sort,' she warned him, more in fear than anger. 'I've got one out there already, remember.'

His reply was cut away by the bell clanging on the board; time for her to help him up the stairs to bed. When she got back Sam had gone.

She left his breakfast to get cold on the table in the servants' hall; let him sulk. But he'd taken the early train, home to Aberdeenshire. She heard nothing, and assumed he was with someone else's horses. How she missed him.

He was back a fortnight later, in the uniform of the Gordons, lifting her feet from the kitchen floor. The laird came through to say how well he looked. A week later he was sent out. She wrote every night, finding it hard to fill a page with the day's news, by lamplight now at the kitchen table. When the laird came in, tight, she shoved the sheet into the drawer. She got replies, flower-bordered cards showing the beauties of France, not a soldier in sight. She had to watch that the Master didn't get to the post first.

At last he was getting leave. Could he come to Invernevis for a couple of days? She wasn't going to ask the laird. Like her brother, Sam still had his place waiting. Anyway, the only thing the laird could remember was an empty cellar.

55

This time his kilt hung as if it was made of lead. His face seemed to have aged; he was always looking around, stubbing out a cigarette after a few draws. She had to give him the second packet.

'Let's climb up to the standing stones,' he suggested.

It was an eerie place the locals avoided, but it was his last night. Taking his kilt off the barbed wire, she tore it.

The big house looked small and dull, across the river. He was chewing grass.

'You've no idea how it is out there.'

His head was on her lap, her spine against the granite pillar, the heat of the day coming through. 'You mustn't talk about it, Sam.' It wasn't only for his sake; she'd enough worry already, with her brother God knows where.

'I don't like leaving you,' he said.

'I'll be all right.' She hugged his head.

His eyes were in the sky.

'Leaving you with him. I thought he was going to fall down this afternoon.'

'I can manage him,' she said factually. She didn't like discussing the Master, not even with Sam.

'He could get out of hand. I went through last night, after the bell. I saw the bugger putting his arm round your waist on the stairs.'

She was shaking. She wanted to push his head away. It wasn't only taking the liberty of saying it against the Master. But it was his last night, and she didn't want a quarrel, especially when he was so nervous.

'He was only steadying himself from falling,' she said, though it had been difficult to remove his arm once they'd reached his room.

She thought that had satisfied him. Then he said: 'I need something of yours to take back with me, to make it bearable.'

She hesitated, then lifted her hands, opening her blouse at the throat. 'Sit up,' she told him.

She poured the delicate chain with the celtic silverwork cross into his palm: a present from the Master, for the years of service.

'It's something else,' he said, his fist closing.

'That's the most precious thing I have,' she said; then understood as his arm went round her waist.

He went north to see his parents. She felt guilty about leaving the Master alone, but couldn't tell him why.

'I'll come to Edinburgh with you, Maggie. We both need a holiday.'

He stayed at his club. She was at the station a good hour before Sam's train was due to pass through from Aberdeenshire. It was dead on time, but nobody was getting out. Hands were reaching out of the windows, but the doors had been locked. They were Gordons.

She ran back and forth, looking for him. There he was, waving. But there were so many women fighting to speak to their men at too few windows. Maggie had to cling with both hands to a handle.

His head was fighting with another one to get out.

'I'm going to desert!'

'No – you *mustn't*!' She was trying to stretch up to his mouth, to stop him from saying it again. Others would be hearing. There was commotion further along, with a woman trying to haul a soldier out of a window. His head and shoulders had stuck. Truncheons were beating him back.

The truncheons came pounding along the side of the train. They were beating Maggie's knuckles.

'Get back, damn you, woman! Back!'

She tried to hang on, but there was blood, and Sam's face had gone. The train lurched and she fell back.

Then she was running beside it with the other women, screaming and using their fists. But the platform suddenly ran out under her shoes.

Several field postcards; everything but I AM QUITE WELL scored out. She wrote, but didn't tell him she was expecting. No answer, not even a postcard. She was sure he'd deserted. It didn't matter if he was with a French girl, as long as he was safe. It was the one thing she couldn't bring herself to discuss with the Master, who had taken to sitting in the kitchen now, with his decanter between them.

But she did ask, vaguely, about what happened to deserters.

'They get what they deserve,' he said, then saw her face. 'Don't worry, Maggie, your brother's too brave to do that kind of thing.'

'He was in the third battle of Ypres,' Father MacInnes said at her back.

She nodded. That meant he was no deserter.

'His medical records were destroyed, but he seems to have been wounded early in the morning of the first day. His company had a hopeless position, in the front line. They would have brought him back here, to the dressing station. Strange, but Vlamertinge was where he camped with the Gordons before going into battle.'

Maggie looked around. Vlamertinge. It had such a sinister sound, but it was a lovely place, with the cemetery so well kept. She was glad she hadn't brought flowers; roses climbed round Sam's stone.

'Those are the spires of Ypres, over yonder.'

But she didn't raise her eyes.

'Don't you feel now that you should tell Iain, Maggie?'

But what did it matter who his father was? It was how he himself had turned out, and both men would have been proud. There were some things you had to take to the grave with you.

'I'm going to say a little prayer, Maggie.'

She bowed her hat while the priest gave thanks for a life he'd known nothing about. But she would never have managed herself.

'I'll wait in the car; take your time.'

Having taken it, she was in no hurry. When she was alone she turned to the monument with the raised sword in the centre of the small cemetery. She sat on the ledge, unlacing someone else's shoes. Then she pulled the long pin from her hat and laid that down too.

She went back to his stone, the evening sun round her latticed stockings; soothing. She pulled other pins, her hair tumbling down, a rope to her waist.

'There you are, Sam; I promised.'

THE SPIDER

Jane Webster

Last night I had a dream.

I was out in the garden, following a trail of dull red moonlight. The foxgloves and delphiniums had been trodden to the ground, and I noticed that their splintered stems dripped blood, not sap. The nest I watched the wrens build had been ripped apart, the chicks split open and turned inside out.

I followed this trail calmly, with something of the detachment of dreams, almost knowing before I found it what the next atrocity would be. It led me full circle round my massacred garden, back into the house that I knew I had left only minutes before. Yet I was not surprised by the holocaust that met me.

My dog was with me, terrified, heart pounding against my legs. But being in the strange underwater world of dreams I was unable to stop and comfort her, only to keep moving, to follow the trail, so that at last I could come face to face with the monstrosity that had destroyed my creation.

It was the noise I heard first, the scrabbling of claws on the bare oak boards. And then I missed the pounding warmth that should have been beside me. I looked at my dog, at the thick black blood welling from her ribs, her legs still twitching as if, at the last, she had abandoned all her years of faithfulness and tried to run. And then I looked at the knife weaving and twisting between my hands and thought, yes, this must have been me.

*

I awoke and all was as it should be, the house undisturbed in its slumber. Only the curtains sidled uneasily at the open window, as if they too had shared a glimpse of my dream. My husband

59

was lying beside me, just as he should be, back turned towards me, one arm thrown over the thickening ribcage so his hand curled into a fist beside his mouth. Strangely vulnerable. His breath had the slow and regular rhythm of genuine sleep. He had not been disturbed by my dream. Yes, everything was just as it should be.

Except that I lay awake, watching the first blue light yawn and stretch its way into the house, appalled that I had allowed it to escape, to come even this far.

In this garden I have created something quite rare. Our visitors comment on its grace and tranquillity, the interweaving of rare and cultivated species. It is a green haze of a garden, broken here and there by a splash of white iris, a pool of yellow celandine. All summer it is haunted by the fragrance of a hedge of tares and honeysuckle, growing together like lovers.

Like them. But my husband is working tonight, sitting in some library examining sixteenth-century tracts on witchcraft. So he has told me, and so I will take care to remember. Just as he will take care to return not too ridiculously late, and I will take care to be in bed by then, sound asleep after a long day in the garden. At least I can give him the relief of not having to lie. He never was an imaginative man.

*

I have never been scared of spiders. Indeed, I quite like them, can sympathize with their scuttling indignation when they have inadvertently fallen into my bath. I always rescue them, place them outside the window so they can recover their self-esteem in the privacy of the wisteria.

In the shed where I keep my gardening tools, a spider has just started to spin her web. Good Scot that I am, I watched her today for half an hour, hoping perhaps that some moral enlightenment would follow. It didn't.

Mine is a slow and meticulous spider, not given like Bruce's to foolhardy leaps. Her plan is well formed and simple, and she follows it exactly, checking each strand as it is completed, running her slender forelegs along the tautened gossamer so that I can almost hear it singing like steel.

The gossamer is secreted from the centre of her abdomen. Does she remain attached when the web is complete, so that her creation becomes a network of live nerves, an extension of herself?

I shall ask my husband. It is the sort of thing he neither knows nor cares about, but it is a conversation piece, a lifeline to throw between us, over the silence that mocks too dangerously our old silence of intimacy.

*

I have taken to watching my face, and am relieved to find that there is no significant change. The fine lines around my eyes, the strands of grey in my hair, are the just consequence of living for forty years, nothing else. As far as I can see there are no cracks or fissures through which any unguarded emotion could escape.

Summer progresses. We continue along the knife edge of our common life, careful to show each other no neglect or discourtesy, treading carefully lest the ground sound hollow under our feet. I walk each day beside the river, my dog running around me in ever widening circles, chasing the wind that somersaults through the corn like dolphins in an emerald sea. I weed the garden, plant out seedlings that will surpass the flowers now in their prime. I gather herbs, dry rose-petals, pluck elderflowers for wine. In short, I check that there is no flaw, no invasion of unease in the peace I have created.

My spider has finished her web. It is perfect, taut and brilliant as youth. This morning it was limned with dew, catching and refracting the early sun like crystal. My spider hovered at the edge, shy as a girl at her first dance, occasionally touching a strand of gossamer as that girl would touch her hair, unable to believe in its beauty.

And my husband still returns for the evening meal, still returns not too ridiculously late. Last night he made love to me, either apologetically or reluctantly, I couldn't tell which. Possibly both. At his climax, his head safely buried in my shoulder, I tried to piece together the woman held behind his tight shut eyes. But I could see and feel nothing.

61

After he was asleep, I lay awake, wondering what this might signify. A phone slammed down in anger, a back turned towards him as he retreats, red-faced and sore from the stinging words? A permanent or a temporary end? Or perhaps it was otherwise; perhaps there was some committal to her that necessitates some valedictory gesture to me. Perhaps my sentence will be delivered to me tomorrow. Or maybe this is nothing but the next strand in our elaborate web of lies.

Either way it must be accepted. All I can do is wait.

*

Tragedy. A butterfly, rose drunk, has blundered into my spider's web.

I found them there this morning, the butterfly exhausted, still spasmodically fluttering his wings as if he believed this to be some nightmare, that presently he would again fly free, out into the sunshine.

My spider was frantic, running hither and thither, thrown into total confusion by the havoc the butterfly had created of her beautiful web, the substitution of this matted, sticky mess for her clear straight lines.

And I myself felt some confusion, some very atypical indecisiveness. To save the butterfly I would have to snap the spider's web. Would that hurt her? Kill her even? I am sure she could not build another web. But why should the butterfly be sacrificed? And the web is already a shambles.

Eventually I picked up my trowel and gloves, and left the shed, shutting the door behind me. It is always best to leave nature to run its course.

*

The butterfly is dead, wings shredded by the twisted lines of gossamer. But the spider has made no move towards him. She huddles at the edge of her warped web, surveying its ruin. Perhaps the web is so distorted that the messages reaching her make no sense. Or perhaps she is scared to move, scared that her movement will finally snap the web.

*

My husband is home. He sits in a chair, staring out the window, staring at the sunlight as if it were unattainable.

And I stand here at the doorway, watching him, scared to ask him if a spider can escape from its own web.

TERRITORY

Ian Rankin

We were in Bordeaux for the summer, teaching English to the unsophisticated sons and daughters of the rich. Poor ourselves, we tried to ignore the small, airless rooms of our *pension* with their peeling wallpaper and rickety furnishings. Having the vague, confident look of tourists, and speaking English, we would breeze in through the etched glass doors of the Excelsior, one of the city's most exclusive hotels, sitting in the air-conditioned lounge reading the English newspapers, sneaking up to the bathrooms on the second floor for showers, baths, shaves.

Ally was the difficult one. The porters and desk clerks worried about his harsh, resonant voice, inflexions galore, and about his dress. Ally was from Edinburgh, and wore nothing less than a Heart of Midlothian football strip in the dazzled heat of the Bordeaux streets. In the cooling evening, a maroon and white scarf might be tied around his neck, irritating his sunburn. The hotel staff were worried about Ally, worried because he refused to play the game of at least trying to look as though he belonged to the general *milieu* of the place.

It was a grand hotel by any standards, set just off the city centre, towards the railway station with its creeping, shadowy nightlife, and the immutable hubbub of the docks. Yet the hotel also retained something of Bordeaux's decadence, its walls stained, the surfaces filmy to the touch. We sipped Cokes in the cocktail bar, feasting on an endless supply of crisps and nuts. Ally and Sue sat together, she feeding him by dropping the tidbits into his yawning mouth, while Christopher and I sat a little apart, not saying much at first, then, as happens, opening up to one another almost as though we had nothing to fear.

Christopher had been nervous at first, deferential, the only

Englishman among three Scots and the population of France. He, too, had applied for the job through a newspaper advertisement. He, too, admitted to being second-rate.

'I can't think why we were chosen.' His eyes watched hungrily as Ally's mouth angled itself beneath Sue's outstretched fingers.

'We were all ready to take the job on their terms,' I answered. The terms were ridiculous. Fifty pounds a week – half of the money in francs – for teaching five days a week, seven hours a day. The preparation for the classes should have taken up most of our weekends, Bordeaux in any case having little enough to offer by way of entertainment, but Ally soon changed that. Within a fortnight of our arrival we had the best five-a-side football team in the area (thanks mainly to two of Ally's students, who were near-professional players), and we had transport in the shape of a battered but unbloody *deux chevaux* (courtesy of another student). We would travel out to the coast and have picnics on the sand dunes at Lacanau-Océan, sometimes begging loans of surfboards, sometimes sunbathing. Ally and Sue used the local nudist beach, but Christopher and I preferred to walk along the coastline, exchanging stories.

His father had died over the course of a painful winter, and he had decided to take a year out from university, sitting at home mostly, listening to his mother play the piano or water her house-plants. Both mother and son were afraid of making too much noise. They did not speak to one another.

'That isn't to say that I don't love her.'

'Of course.'

'What about you?'

But I had nothing to tell. Back at the beach, Africans, wildly overdressed in the heat, were trying to sell the nudists bangles and ice creams. No one was buying, but they continued to stalk their territory, afraid of failure. And back at the Hotel Excelsior, an old man was moving slowly up the smooth-worn steps, accompanied by a young girl in white.

*

Christopher brought two glasses of wine across to our table in the hotel bar, while I finished one bowl of peanuts and started on another. Ticky, one of the African waiters, who took pity on us despite his own eighteen-hour shifts, came across to the table grinning. He had brought with him another bowl of nuts from a vacant table.

'You must keep up your strength,' he said, still grinning. 'You have not seen the new English lady yet.'

At that, a shuffling sound announced the arrival of an elderly man into the bar. Ticky nodded towards him, then winked at us. The girl followed the old man to a barren table. She manoeuvred him into one of the deep armchairs, and seated herself on the edge of another, looking around her. Christopher and I smiled. She looked away as if in utter boredom.

'What a cracker,' whispered Christopher close by my ear.

She was in her late teens, pale and slim, made paler and slimmer by a white cotton dress, fringed with lace. Her hair, however, was thick and dark, falling in waves from a centre parting, and her lips were a lipstick red, though she was not wearing lipstick. Ticky winked again.

Walking to our *pension* through the sticky late-evening streets, streets of the most genteel poverty, we couldn't help but talk about the girl. There were few enough topics of conversation left to us: how could we let her escape?

'She must be his daughter,' said Christopher.

'Or his niece.'

'Or granddaughter?'

'Yes, most likely his granddaughter.'

They had spoken little in the bar, she sipping a long, orange drink while he threw back six or seven cognacs. When he spoke, his voice was loudly, properly that of the Englishman abroad, self-conscious of lost empires and trying to disguise the fact. Whether the girl spoke to him or merely moved her lips we could not decide from our table.

'Nothing else, surely. I mean, it can't be anything more than that, can it?'

The small, rounded glasses of cognac had brought a ruddy vigour to the man's face, and especially to his forehead, which highlighted the slick silver hair above it. When he ran his fingers over his head, a sprig of hair would make a show of protest, standing out from the rest until the girl's fingers coaxed it back into place. He chuckled as she did this, his eyes becoming slits among so much puffed flesh. Then he asked for and was brought a telephone, and took a tiny notebook from his pocket, holding the pages up close to his face.

Looking back, he should have been dressed in a white three-piece suit, with a silver-tipped cane, a watch-chain, and perhaps a wide-brimmed hat. He deserved no less, but was in fact wearing a short-sleeved shirt and casual trousers, with plimsolls on his feet where the handbeaten leather shoes should have been. Even dressed like this, however, he fitted into the expensive bar as though trained for the part, or rather, as though *it* had been trained especially for him. His attitude towards the girl had not been particularly paternal.

'A secretary?'

'Not quite efficient enough, and not nearly flash enough.'

A horn sounded behind us then, and the low, dangerous roar of Ally's foot on the accelerator heralded the drunken *deux chevaux* containing Ally and two of his students.

'Just been on the phone to my mum,' he shouted through the window. 'My little sister's gotten herself engaged to her boss. How do you like that?'

As we made to move off, Christopher pointed to a chauffeured car which passed us. Two figures were embracing in its back seat.

'It's ridiculous,' said Ally. 'She's fifteen years younger than him. My mum's furious.'

The students laughed at this for some reason, and Ally stared at them, then began to laugh himself.

*

Janice's pale skin turned almost pellucid over the course of the next few weeks, the veins and arteries beneath pulsing with what seemed slower and slower life. We had all become friends of a sort, after one blustering evening in the near-empty bar. The old gentleman had something to celebrate, and we were

his thick, manicured nails. The conversation had turned into another silence, and beyond this particular silence lay only argument. It was time for me to leave.

*

He was to spend a day visiting some of the oldest private vineyards in the Medoc. It was something of an honour, he was told, and not to have gone might have prejudiced several of the deals he had been busily working out in the comfort of the Hotel Excelsior.

It was a day of giddy, numbing heat, and we were all going to the coast. The classes were winding up, and we were planning our separate jaunts around Europe. Bill grumbled a lot, sensing the danger, but finally allowed Janice to come with us to Lacanau-Océan. He pulled me to one side beforehand and more or less offered me a job with his company in London if I was careful to look after Janice and see that she returned to him. His eyes were feverish. I told him not to forget to wear a hat on his visit to the vineyards.

'And try not to touch any of the '77. It's garbage.'

The beach outside Lacanau was busy, but further away from the town, past the dunes and the nudist beach, we found a quieter stretch of gritty sand, and staked our claim to it. Janice was so painfully slender in her bikini that we wondered whether she would have the strength to make it down to the water's edge. She did, and as the day progressed and the heat grew more debilitating, she seemed to grow stronger. Colour began pounding through her body, and she laughed and shrieked, shouted even, as we played in the water, swimming well while Christopher trod water and watched with his thin, calculating eyes.

We had bread, salami, cheese and two bottles of wine in a cool-box. While we ate, Janice told us about herself, hesitantly at first, but then more animatedly, growing in confidence as she saw that she had caught our interest. She had been fifteen when she had met Bill – a friend of her uncle. She had run away with him at sixteen, moving from Lincoln to London, but gradually spending more and more time abroad.

'It was all a great adventure at first, I suppose. He was a real charmer, pots of money. We had a lot of fun. Casinos, country houses, all that. But he's become, I don't know, different. Almost as if he's running scared. We come abroad lots, I think because he's afraid I'll run away from him, and he knows I'm less likely to do that in a foreign country than in London.' She traced a delicate pattern in the sand, as though the sand were flesh.

'Do you want to leave him?' Christopher swallowed hard, aware of a slight but noticeable edge in his voice. Janice stared at him, and then at us all.

'I don't know,' she said. 'Sometimes ...'

'Get shot of him,' said Ally, tearing at a crust of bread. 'He's too old for you. He's taking advantage.'

'Oh, come off it, Ally, that's hardly – ' As Christopher had done, I swallowed now, desperate not to be seen to take sides.

'He seems nice enough,' said Sue. 'He doesn't hurt you or anything, Janice?'

'Oh no, never. He's always kind, but it's not kindness for the sake of kindness.'

'That's the rich for you, love,' spat Ally. 'Always an ulterior motive. That's why you should leave him.'

'You could come with us.' Christopher was wiping sand from his burning arms. 'We're all leaving the day after tomorrow. It would be easy. Just walk out of the hotel, that's all.'

Yes, Christopher had his plans, plans so similar to Bill's own that I wanted suddenly to grab him by the shoulders and shake him.

'I suppose I could do that,' said Janice quietly, 'if I wanted to. Couldn't I?'

Ally put his arm around Sue's neck, drawing her further towards him. 'And don't you go getting any ideas about stepping into Janice's shoes. No rich sugar-daddies for you, love. Only poor old me to look after.'

A distant figure, plodding ever nearer, became a sweating, burdened African, selling bangles and ice creams. We shook our heads guiltily, and he turned without speaking, heading back towards the dunes with his load.

*

71

Bill lay in bed, the coverlet around his waist, while one of the hotel staff daubed at his face with a cold cloth. We had returned to the hotel purposely late, a sign of Janice's independence, having stopped off at a restaurant for a meal and some drinks. Bill looked deathly pale, and closed his eyes on the vision of Janice, glowing with health and youth. His eyes rested on me finally and as if in judgement, while the African waiter explained that the *monsieur* had been taken ill at one of the vineyards, the heat most certainly being to blame. A doctor had been called for. All would be well.

Janice sat on the bed and held Bill's hand, but he could not bear to look at what we had made of her, his face dissolved into the lines of so many years spent living.

I visited him the next day after breakfast. He was sitting in the lounge – out of bed against the advice of the doctor – and was busy with a telephone. He ordered tea for us, and told me that Janice was in her room.

'Don't do this to me,' he said quietly, his eyes on the telephone. 'I can say that to you. You understand, don't you?'

'Yes,' I said, sipping tea, 'I think so.'

'Why is that?' His eyes narrowed. 'Why is it that you understand while others never could?'

Outside the doors of the hotel, traffic slowly pushed its way into the heart of the city like fluid from a syringe. The tourist season was at its height. People drifted up to the reception desk, full of questions, their French brutally correct. Kate had spoken eloquent, poetic French when away from the classroom.

'I'm not here for the fun of it, you know.' I pinched the skin between my eyes, trying to look burdened. 'We're all here to hide from something, aren't we? Even Ally, though God knows what it is that *he's* running away from.'

'And you?' His eyes were tender now, wise and vulnerable. They made me feel younger than my years, a child in shorts seated on his great-uncle's knees, making up stories.

'I was in love with an older woman,' I began, 'back in Jedburgh.' My eyes were on the gabble of tourists at the reception desk. 'It's a small place. You can't hide that sort of thing.' How could he be expected to understand what was an essentially Scottish problem? He was from London, from high society. He had never experienced the womb-warmth of a small town, all those surrogate mothers, fathers, uncles and aunts, met every time you went into a shop or stepped onto a bus. 'My parents – well, my mother – she was furious. The woman, Kate, had been my French teacher at one time. My mother threatened her, threatened her whole career. And Kate broke it off between us.'

'So you came here?'

'I was offered the job. I thought, what the hell.'

'You came here to get over Kate?'

He had not understood. 'God, no. Not Kate. I came here to find out how I felt about my mother, about my whole town. I came here to find out whether I could ever go back.'

'And?' I shrugged my shoulders, while Bill poured more tea. 'And so,' he went on, 'you can sympathize with my own ... feelings?'

'I suppose so.' I wanted to burst out of the hotel's gleaming doors, to push my way through the crowds of shoppers, running towards the cold rushing sea, the seemingly eternal coastline.

'But you will still take her away from me, won't you?'

'Nobody's *taking* anything!'

The people at reception looked over at us. Bill stroked the telephone. His notebook lay on the table beside us, crammed with names and telephone numbers, written in pencil in a tiny script. Suddenly I remembered the sort of man he was: businesslike, calculating, manipulative. What did Janice mean to him? I knew the answer to that. She meant life itself, because he had foolishly come to believe in the tales he had heard, and believing in them made them come true.

'It doesn't matter,' he said, lifting the receiver, and it was as if the telephone weighed several pounds as he tried to bring it to his ear.

*

Christopher brought her down the steps, her case in his left hand, her arm in his right. He looked very pleased with himself, having insisted on going into the hotel alone. Ally revved the engine: the car was his for another month, and Sue and he intended driving south to Provence. Christopher was going along with them, and so, I assumed, was Janice. She was wearing a white shawl over her shoulders, and was smiling. First, however, they would drop me off at the station.

But Janice had, she told us, decided to return to England. Bill had given her the money – quite a lot of it – over dinner on the previous evening. Christopher suddenly seemed interested in the car's tiny dashboard, but said nothing.

'Well in that case,' said Ally, 'we'll drop you at the station with Ian. You can travel together. Perfect.'

Sue smiled at Janice, and Janice smiled at me, and we moved away from the Hotel Excelsior, waving back to Ticky, who had appeared on the steps. There was no sign of Bill, and Janice said that he had gone out before breakfast.

'I told you it would be easy,' yelled Ally over the engine.

At the railway station, after hugs, kisses and handshakes, we watched the *deux chevaux* pull away, kicking up dust and grit, heading along the waterfront. Janice smiled at me again.

'Well,' I said, looking around me, trying out the role of temporary guardian, 'the ticket office is through here, I think.' I started to lift our cases, but her hand stopped me.

'Let's sit out here for a little while. It's nice.'

It was not particularly 'nice'. There were some late-morning drunks and ravaged-looking teenagers sitting on the ground nearby, and the only bench had to be shared with a small, snoring woman with wrinkled stockings hanging around her ankles. Janice did not seem keen to talk, though she continued to smile serenely. I reasoned that this morning had been something of an upheaval for her, and that her silence was quite in order. I thought, too, of Bill, wasting away in his shackles of luxury, empty without her. He was learning a late lesson, perhaps. And what of me? Was I returning home, or moving further away? I still did not know. Just then Janice sprang to her feet, grabbing my hand. The chauffeured car had slowed to a halt in front of us.

'Here he is,' she said. 'Come on.' She had picked up her case, and as a figure inside the car leaned forward to push open the back door, I found myself picking up my own heavy pack and following.

74

AMERICAN DREAM

Maureen Monaghan

The last of the winter daylight still spread a weak golden stain over the middle of the carpet, but the corners of the room were already dark. Angus shifted his weight from one aching buttock to the other, and groaned. It started as a long sigh from the depths of his chest, but he opened his mouth and gave it voice, and Effie came running from the kitchen. The florid overstuffed room was hot, the air thick with stewed tea and disinfectant, secretly rancid with the smells of his helplessness. Soon, she would draw the curtains, and it would be just the two of them and the foolish technicolour chatter from Aberdeen and the click of her knitting needles. Angus groaned because always, as the long day slid, wasted, into the long night, Effie would come through from the kitchen saying, 'Now, Dad, don't you fret. We'll have a last wee look out of the window before I shut the curtains. Then we'll be nice and cosy at the fire. Just you and me and the telly. 'Till bedtime.'

Effie, with her sandy hair and red hands and glowing, homely face.

She fussed around the fireplace, riddling and poking, stabbing the smouldering slabs of peat into trickles of flame. The brass fire-irons tinkled as she replaced them on their stand in the hearth. She went into the kitchen for a tray of scones, hot from the oven, which she showed to him, before putting them out in the porch to cool. 'We'll have a fine tea tonight, then, Dad!'

Effie, born old, feeding puppies and kittens and broken-winged birds when she was only a bairn herself.

She tilted back the old wheelchair, tucking the fringes of his rug clear of the dusty fragile spokes, and pushing him over to the window. She leaned on the handle of the chair, like a gossip

75

leaning over a gate, forgetting to put the two firm legs back on the floor. Angus could only see the line of bare trees against the bleak storm-filled sky, while his neglected fields were on a plane below his vision. He asked if it was the gales that had finished off the two sycamores over at Brathens Farm. She rocked him up and down in the chair. He said he had heard that the Council would make Jamie Baillie give up half his field when they straightened the road. She bent over and wiped his wet mouth. 'Wheesht, Dad! Don't you worry about the storm. I'll look after you.'

Effie, carrying the messages for his beloved ailing May, calling, 'Come on, Mam, we'll be soaked if you don't walk faster. Hurry up, now!'

She edged the clumsy chair round from the window and wheeled him to the fireside. She went back to stare at the icy rain slicing across the grey and yellow sky. Angus leaned back in the chair away from the heat. He told her to come away from the window, to move him, he was too hot. She said, 'Hush, now! I know you don't like the rain. I won't let you get wet, Dad!'

Effie, shouting to him in the potato patch, 'Dada! Mam's fallen down in the path and hit her head. We'll have to get her in out of the rain!'

Angus, red and struggling, wondered what she could see in the darkening garden. Often she gave directions to lost motorists or to travellers looking for accommodation. She would go through the glassed-in porch to the front door, keeping him out of sight in the living-room. She would chat about busy routes and short cuts, and the roadworks near Aboyne and the new hotel at Braemar. She would offer cups of tea. She would walk with the caller down the path to the roadside, saying, 'I won't be long, Dad! It's my Dad. He doesn't get about much. Since the stroke. Terrible shame! You'd think they could do something.'

Effie, telling young Nurse Black not to go upsetting her Dad with talk of hospitals and exercises and big shiny wheelchairs that could go round corners, like motor cars.

At last she left the window and pulled his chair back from the

76

fire. She put on the lights – the yellowed fringed standard lamp on one side of the hearth, and the angled chrome on top of the television on the other side. The blackness outside was dense. She started to close the curtains. 'Goodness, Dad, I think we've got a visitor. Coming up the path. He must be soaked. I'd best ask him in. Good thing I made all those scones!' And she bustled away, smoothing her apron and patting her wispy hair.

Angus heard a whoosh of wind and rain as she opened the porch door. 'Oh, you poor soul, you're wringing! Give me that big wet coat. I'll put the electric on in the front room. You'll be warm in no time. Your car's broken? Now don't worry about that. We'll see about it when the rain stops.'

He heard her switching things on in the room they never used now. He thought of May's fine embroidered chairbacks, and his mother's stitched message, framed and hung on the wall: 'Jesus Loves Me. Euphemia Jane Scott. 1903'.

'Come in and sit down,' said Effie. 'It's a nice wee room, isn't it! My Dad won those at the Games, you know.' Angus knew she polished the shapely silver cups every week. 'I'll just tell him you're here. No, he won't come in. He's not well. He won't speak to anyone but me, he's so shy.'

> Effie, screaming at the district nurse, 'Stop telling such lies, Grace Black! You know fine he can't talk! There's no sense in his drooling, and you know it!'

She came in and gave Angus his supper, gentle as she spooned in the soft, eggy mess, then the bits of buttered scone. 'He's an American, Dad. You should see the big car he's got. And the big fur collar on his coat. He works with the oil-rigs.' She gave him hot sweet tea from the feeding-cup. 'Now I'll put the telly on for you, Dad, while I take something to Mr Bloomberg. That's his name. Wayne Jay Bloomberg. Isn't that a nice name, Dad? Americans always have nice names.'

> Effie, home from her first day at school, lisping, 'The teacher said Euphemia Mary was too big for a wee girl and she would just call me Effie. That's a nice name, isn't it, Dada?'

She went to and fro between the kitchen and the living-room press, gathering scones and tea and the best china. 'He must be hungry, Dad, after his car breaking down in all that rain.' She moved his chair nearer the television and put a cushion behind his head. 'There's cowboys soon, Dad. You like that. I'll away and look after the visitor. It's nice to have someone to talk to!'

When the fire was a heap of fine ash, and the blank screen hummed quietly, Angus began to rock his stiff body in the wheelchair. He could hear her soft murmur from the front room. 'My Dad needs me here, Mr Bloomberg. I'd like to go to America with you, but I couldn't leave him. If you see my Mam, tell her we miss her. She went away to America a long time ago, Mr Bloomberg.'

Angus roared, 'Your Mam's dead, lassie! She never went anywhere but six feet under. Oh, it was a sin for me to tell such stories to a daft bairn. Take her to America, Wayne J. Bloomberg. Take her as far away as you like. Nurse Grace will be here in the morning. We'll manage fine.'

Effie, sobbing into his black sleeve, 'Why did Mam go to America without us, Dada? Who'll look after us now?'

She hurried into the living-room, and wiped his wet mouth and his old tear-filled eyes. 'Ssh, Dad! I'll not go to America and leave you. Don't you upset yourself.'

Effie, crooning to her dolls, 'Don't cry, babies. When I'm big, I'll take you all to America with me. I'll not leave you. Effie will always look after you.'

NORIKA

Peter Regent

'Hai!' cried Miss Ikoshi, her delicate lips parted in a smile. 'Hai!', and she nodded vigorously.

Murdoch bayed more imbecilities, and invited her to laugh. Miss Ikoshi laughed, formally but musically. 'Hai!' she cried again, and her neat head rocked to and fro on the perfect fulcrum of her astonishingly vertical neck, as if it were worked by wires. 'Hai' is the Japanese for 'yes', and Miss Ikoshi was affirming so emphatically that the sound came out as 'hah!'.

'Hah! Haha!' gasped Miss Ikoshi, and Murdoch looked at me sideways with a lascivious curl to the corners of his mouth.

That started the game. Without exchanging a word, Murdoch and I set out to make remarks that caused Miss Ikoshi to cry 'Hah! Haha! Hahaha!', till her panting climax turned all the heads in the bar and made the barman stop serving and come to our end of the counter to see whether this public orgasm required his intervention.

Afterwards I felt bad about it. Of course, Murdoch had started it, but I needn't have joined in, especially as I didn't like him much and Miss Ikoshi was technically my guest. No doubt I was vexed with her for being so taken up with him. Murdoch had no business appropriating her, and she – whose first name he had brusquely demanded – had no business letting herself be appropriated. I supposed culture-shock had something to do with that; her code of manners probably required that if Murdoch was patronizing she was obliged to gasp ardent assent to his chatter, and she was very well-mannered.

But she was my discovery. It was I who had started going to the small art school that was housed in the university museum and open to undergraduates by the terms of its foundation. There were full-time painting students as well, most of them young women who had been sent there in lieu of a finishing school. The address was good, and the girls had excellent opportunities for meeting well-heeled undergraduates without the tedious requirement of written entrance examinations or any pretence of verbal study. I must admit that several of them were quite good painters, and have since gone on to make respectable reputations as interior designers and so forth, but what impressed me most at the time was their clothes. I was insensitive to fine points of cut or quality, but even I could see that their dresses and suits, worn with high heels and stockings and casually risked in a studio where every surface was a possible support for wet paint, were not the same as shopgirls wore. In pencil-slim silk slacks and smocks they still looked wanly elegant after far later nights – judging from their conversation – than most undergraduates could afford. Deeply captivated as I was by the fleshy architecture of the model on the stand, the clothed and unattainable body of Celia – or Julia, or Tania, or Philippa – could distract me from my investigation of nakedness. But Miss Ikoshi's arrival was the biggest distraction of all.

I had grown out of my childhood impression that Japanese women were delicate creatures modelled in glib porcelain or undulating and smirking like the figures in westernized prints. Wartime photographs, the films that were just beginning to arrive, and occasional sightings in the street had suggested that all Japanese were tawny-skinned, muscular and more or less bow-legged. Miss Ikoshi corrected my over-correction. Apart from her western clothes, she might have stepped from a *Kano* screen or an Utamaro print – except that her face was no courtesan's mask. Her cheeks were bright, not rice-powdered – though her skin was too incredibly fine for everyday wear in this rough world – and there was nothing enervated about the fall of her full skirt. Moreover, the legs that emerged from it and proceeded, through admirably turned ankles, to the ballet slippers then fashionable, were straight, in the pleasantly curved way that legs are straight.

Since I was in my second year, I could spare one and sometimes two afternoons a week for painting. After Miss Ikoshi

arrived I regularly spared two, and sometimes three. I
exchanged apologies with her as we brushed past each other in
the narrow space between the easels and the back wall. If our
eyes accidentally met across the room we smiled politely. I
spied on her during the model's rest, when she looked at other
people's work and sighed admiration. I looked at hers and
found a curious linear robustness.

'It's rather good,' I said. 'Do you know the work of Foujita?'

'I know of him, but prease, I am trying to be a painter, not a
Japanese painter.'

I understood, I assured her, and looked wisely at her canvas.
'Oil isn't much used in Japan, is it?'

'More so now. We must be part of wor'd art.'

After a few more banalities I moved away. It was a start.
Only it was also very nearly the end of term, and when we
reassembled I found I really couldn't afford the three pound ten
art school fee. Consequently I did not see Miss Ikoshi again
until one afternoon when I was idling away an hour in the
museum that housed the art school in its basement, like a single
living toe under a mummy's windings.

Actually, the analogy is not entirely fair to the museum,
which was a rather good one, full of treasures, but always
deserted, except for the occasional old lady gloating over the
porcelain. Wandering through its unguarded halls gave one a
pleasant sensation of trespassing. I walked softly, and quite
surprised Miss Ikoshi, where she stood quietly irradiating the
Uccello, of which the museum is justly proud, with her beauty.

'They've labelled it "A hunting scene by night",' I said, 'but
I read somewhere that it's really daytime, and only dark
because it's in the depths of the forest.'

She gave a little burst of surprised laughter, then, 'Hai! I
think that is nicer.'

I saw what she meant. The sense of enclosure gave an added
charm to that gay pattern of limbs, rocking-horse steeds and
arc-en-ciel hounds, arrogant young faces and odd perspectives.
I enjoyed our shared enclosure in the dark forest, filled with the
baying of hounds and winding of horns. 'It's a famous painting,' I said.

'Hai! I rike it *very* much.'

That was the day I first took Miss Ikoshi back to my room for tea. There, over Marks and Spencer crumpets which I had toasted at the electric fire, we exchanged first names. Hers was Norika. Her father was a diplomat, but with very modern ideas; he was anxious that she should mix freely with Europeans and get to understand their ways, so that she could pioneer a role for Japanese women in the development of cultural and business relations with the West. She said it as if it were a lesson.

'It sounds a good idea,' I said.

'Perhaps. But I am not sure that I will be a good dipromat. I prefer painting.'

Since she refused more crumpets, I pressed on her a slice of cake. The fact was that, having enticed this exotic creature into my room, I was not sure what to do with her. Japanese court-ship must certainly involve procedures and rituals of which I knew nothing; I might so easily put a foot wrong and ruin everything – or I might accidentally do something that commit-ted me to supporting a full set of wizened ancestors for ever.

Norika asked about my painting. I said I liked painting people. I had of course already contemplated the possibility of getting her to pose for me, having read somewhere that the Japanese were quite unselfconscious about nudity. The exquis-ite nature of those parts of her that were exposed made the prospect of discovering the rest particularly delightful. Perhaps she would regard it as a normal proposal from a fellow art student – which was more than Julia and Celia and their friends would do. Of course, it would be disastrous if Horace, the staircase scout, were to surprise us when he came to collect the dirty tea things. That made me hesitate, but above all, I doubted whether I could draw her creditably. Recording the chunky palpability of the art school models was one thing; capturing such astringent perfection as Norika's was another. Perhaps I also sensed her vulnerability, and did not want to take advantage.

'You know, I'd like to draw your head,' I said.

Norika blessed the air with her sweet, formal laugh. 'Hai!' she said, 'prease do.'

*

My fears were justified; she was indeed difficult. I struggled, and was beginning to think I might bring my third beginning to something, when there was a knock at the door. It was Murdoch, from one flight down, come to suggest a quick one before dinner. He made no effort to conceal his surprise at seeing Norika, and delivered his invitation with a knowing leer and his eyes fixed on her in sidelong lust.

'Can I see?' He came to look at the drawings, shuffling and smudging them. 'Very nice,' he pronounced, so I was obliged to show them to Norika too, apologizing for not having done her justice. Probably I should have made a graceful compliment of it if we were alone, but Murdoch put me off. 'Japanese girl too tricky, eh?' he said. 'What about this drink, then. Why don't you both come?'

Norika looked pleased – but I had already noticed that politeness seemed to make her look pleased at everything. 'I have never been in a pub,' she said.

'Now's your chance, then,' said Murdoch.

'Would you like to?' I asked.

'Hai!' Norika dipped her head and wasted her formal laugh on Murdoch's red ears. As she got up he beat me to her jacket, which fell gracefully about her shoulders even from his crude hands. On the stairs her ankles scissored neatly. No, she was definitely not bow-legged.

Murdoch followed, breathing coarsely. I did not like him much. He was quite well off, and had been to a lesser public school that left him with a baying voice that did not completely conceal Hertfordshire vowels. Despite his relative prosperity he occasionally found himself a bit short towards the end of term, and he still owed me five pounds. I resented that, and I resented his success with women even more.

In a college of men from single-sex schools, some of whom were probably beginning to doubt what they had heard about human sexual reproduction, Murdoch alone had girls – and had them openly. His success was extraordinary. They came in succession, bearing their ripe bodies across the quad to the altar of his bed. They strutted on high heels, exercised skin-tight trousers, marched sturdy boots that reached to their dimpling knees, and trailed heady perfume like full-blown summer roses; none of them was particularly attractive. It was fairly clear that Murdoch's success was at least partly the result of lack of discrimination. Most people would have avoided being seen with Murdoch's girls, though they might fantasize about them in private. Like Murdoch, they were not quite the thing. One of them had been seen in buttock-flashing shorts in the High Street; another talked loudly about contraception, and another had said 'fuck' over there, by the lodge. No one but Murdoch was in a position to say whether any of them were intellectually interesting, and he did not discuss the matter. He was less reluctant to talk about their physical attributes and only yesterday he had told me, while borrowing some sherry, 'Devina looks a hellish lump when she's dressed, but actually, you know, she's got perfect tits, old man.'

And now, having brought us to White's bar, Murdoch was talking to Norika; asking her name, blundering on about the binding of women's feet and being quite unabashed when it was pointed out that he was confusing China with Japan. No doubt he was trying to detect whether she had perfect tits or not. Now he started to tell her about Lefcadio Hearne, of whom I had not heard, and offering to lend her books. In my resentment I made a desperate throw.

'Would you like to come to the theatre on Thursday?' I asked Norika, in a quiet tone, as if Murdoch were not there.

Norika purified the air that Murdoch had been breathing with her little formal laugh. 'Hai! I should rike that very much,' she said.

*

It was an open-air performance of *Twelfth Night* in a college garden. Norika watched it all, the clowning and the romanticizing, with the same grave attention. They managed to make it rather long, and when I said I supposed the *Noh* plays were even longer she said yes, but this was more like *Kabuki* – only they were longer too. She seemed to have enjoyed it, but by the end she was obviously conscious of the cold that seeped up from the damp grass under the benches. As we walked away towards her lodgings I felt protective, and considered telling her she was

84

like a butterfly that had stayed out too late. I did call her a 'poor mite', and was about to put an arm round her yellow coat when a figure stepped from a doorway. It was Murdoch.

'Going home so soon?'

'That was the idea,' I said.

'Come for a drink.'

'Another time, perhaps. Norika's rather cold and I've got an essay.'

'I know a cosy place with a fire – I'll take you out there in the car.'

'No, really.'

'Your essay'll wait. Or if not go and do it and I'll take Norika for a drink and run her home – she'll love this place, and it's bad for me to drink alone.' He looked pathetically at Norika, and her little laugh came sweetly pat.

'No, really, another time,' I said, annoyed – then added, to Norika, 'unless, of course ...?'

'Oh no, I think.'

'No, go if you want to. It's just that I've got this essay for tomorrow.'

Norika looked from one to the other, obviously anxious to do the right thing in a strange country. It was quite clear to me what that was. 'I think I should take you home,' I said.

Norika smiled at Murdoch and obediently turned to go. After we had walked a little way down the lane she asked, 'He wir not be offended?'

'Not at all.'

'You see, when these things arise I am not sure what is correct.'

'You should just please yourself.' I stopped walking. 'Look, you should go if you want – really.'

'You think I should?'

Annoyed, because I knew she shouldn't but I didn't want to argue about it, I said, 'Perhaps you should,' and shouted after Murdoch, who was walking slowly in the opposite direction.

'Thank you for taking me to the theatre – it was very nice,' said Norika, before Murdoch carried her off. I went home, resentful, but telling myself that, after all, I didn't own the girl.

My mood, and the fact that I didn't hear Murdoch come in – though he must have done so – didn't help with the essay. The sky was paling over the chapel roof when I opened the curtains and went to bed, resigned to extemporizing to Snuffy Carswell yet again.

After that Norika and I saw each other from time to time. We drank coffee in the Cadena, and we went to the pictures – she chose *Quai des Brumes* in preference to *The Seven Samurai*. One day I met her coming across the quad towards my staircase, and was pleased to think that this ethereal creature, so different from the girls from Somerville and St Anne's, with their rosy faces, thick voices and seven-league boots, was coming to see me. 'I'm just dashing to a tutorial,' I said, 'but – '

Norika inspired a blackbird to a cadenza with her laugh. 'It's all right,' she said, 'I was just going to see Adrian.' Adrian was Murdoch. She was entitled to see whom she liked, of course.

But she seemed to enjoy my company too. One hot afternoon I took her punting. As she stepped on the gently swaying duckboards of the punt and arranged herself neatly on the cushions, I glimpsed golden knees, suave in their simplicity and utterly remote from the pink outcrops English girls were exposing on the landing stage. We set off downstream, weaving between other punts. A lout from Christ Church lay back and watched a laughing girl whom he had imported from his county flexing her sturdy body in its blue bathing suit as she swung her pole to race us. The year before I would have been full of admiration and envy, but now I looked down on the loafer with cool superiority, as I swept my superior cargo past. In the green gloom of the upper reaches, where few other punts ventured, Norika and I talked about art, and afterwards we bicycled out to the Trout for tea. It would have been a perfect day, except that Murdoch turned up there.

It seemed evident to me that Norika must, if only because of our common interest in painting, find my conversation more interesting than Murdoch's and – well, I did try to anticipate her uncertainties and help her with meeting people. He always seemed so grossly insensitive that I simply could not understand why she continued to see him. I was in love with her, of course, just as I was in secret love with the crumbling town that was being shaken to bits by the traffic, with the dreaming dons – I hated it when they revealed their underlying worldliness – and even with the handsome, confident young people whom I affected to despise. If I contemplated physical lovemaking with Norika it was only in a vague romantic dream of midnight punting, or college gardens after a ball. I did not calculate.

*

Going upstairs to my room after a virtuous day in the library, I saw that the slabby wooden panel that was usually to one side of Murdoch's doorway had been slid on its runners across the door. Murdoch was sporting his oak. People usually did that only when they were immersed in study and anxious not to be disturbed, and that was hardly likely in Murdoch's case. I was tempted to break the unwritten rule and thump on the heavy brown panels to demand the return of my sherry – for there was a meeting in my room before dinner, and I had forgotten to buy some. But since Murdoch almost certainly had a woman inside, I scribbled on a piece of paper and bent to shove it under the door – only, of course, it wouldn't go, because of the sliding runner. Instead I slipped it between the side of the oak and the inner door, hoping that Murdoch would find it when he emerged. As I did so my suspicions were confirmed by a treble voice. I wondered why Horace never reported that Murdoch had girls in behind his oak, which was a very grave offence. Then I was tempted to find some excuse to fetch him and send him scurrying off to the Dean, for, of course, the voice was Norika's. She was uttering her gasping sounds of affirmation with an ardency that struck me like a blow in the stomach. As I turned away and lurched on up the stairs I heard her exultant, laughing cry.

I thought I should never be able to face Norika again, but when I met her in the High Street she seemed so unselfconscious and natural that I almost thought I must have been mistaken. We went for coffee in the Cadena, and as we sat by the steamed-up windows above the street, in the warm room smelling of buns, I scanned her face for the coarseness that

Murdoch must have implanted there. All was as flawless as ever, and I was sure that she might yet be saved.

'There's something I ought to tell you,' I began.

'Hai?'

I shuddered at the associations of that breathless gasp. 'It's a bit difficult to say, in fact. It's about Murdoch.'

'Did I do something wrong? Is he offended with me?'

I gave an incompetent impression of a man laughing. 'Of course not. Nothing like that, it's just that – well ...' and I told her about Murdoch. I didn't exactly say he was a shit, but I let her know. I laid it on fairly hard, and I added that, though no one really disliked him, no one really respected him either. Of course, she must be wondering why I should be telling her all this – after all, she hardly knew him, but it was a question of her reputation, more than anything else. I really felt rather awful, talking about a chap behind his back like that, but I was conscious that she was in a strange country, and things might not be as obvious to her as they would be to – to – '

'To an Engrish girl?'

I roared with laughter. Yes, to an English girl.

'But I think Adrian knows some Engrish girls.'

I wondered if she had understood all that I had been saying. 'Yes, that's the point. You see – well, no one respects them.'

Norika laughed her formal laugh very briefly. 'I understand. Thank you for terring me.' She looked up, laughed again, and smiled a dazzling smile. 'I shall take care.'

'Yes. Well, good. Would you like some more coffee?'

'No thank you.' There was a pause, then she asked, 'Will you go to the art school again next term?'

'I don't think so. It'll be my final year, you see.'

'I think it is a pity you have stopped going.'

'Well ... ' I shrugged. 'It's not what I'm here for, really.'

We sat in silence for what seemed a long time, and as I secretly looked at her I felt a dull pain at the thought that Murdoch knew what I could only divine – that her slimness was more voluptuous than the imperceptive might expect, that her slight breasts were in fact sleekly and poetically just right, that the contrast between her black hair and the ivory of her body – I brusquely got up to go.

'I think I shall not be here next term.' Norika sat stiffly upright as she spoke.

I sat down again, with the feeling that the sun had gone in outside and it might never reappear. 'How's that?' I asked.

'My father is coming next week. He thinks I should go to study in Paris.'

'But you're settled in here now, and the school's not so bad. You've made friends ... ' I hoped she would understand that I was saying I'd hate it if she went away.

'I must see what my father says.'

I sensed that it would be better not to insist, and had a nasty feeling that I had already made a serious mistake in talking about Murdoch. I groped for something neutral to say.

'So your father's coming?'

'Yes. I hope you wi' see him. He wants to meet my friends.'

*

Mr Ikoshi turned out to be a man between ages. It was not just that he was Japanese and therefore hard to place; it was that he was leaving youth for middle age, and elements of the two stages contended in him. When he laughed it was with less restraint than Norika, and youth dominated; when he sipped wine the older man appeared, savouring with keenly narrowed cheeks and judicial eyes. Both characters were dignified, but the young man was informal where the old man was formidable.

Murdoch and I helped Norika to show him the colleges. Murdoch was rather an embarrassment, and insisted on demonstrating such things as the climbing-in route behind the bike sheds, where a group of the spiked wheels that were fixed to a rail along the top of the college wall each had one spoke missing, so that when they were turned to match one could crawl under them, and when they were set at random the barrier appeared intact. If Mr Ikoshi had any views about grown men using such tricks to get in and out after dark he gave no sign, apart from nodding gravely. Later, as he sat sipping tea with a group of art school girls sitting on the floor around him, and Norika kneeling by the tea things, he was a patrician figure. Whenever he did not understand something that was said, his question to Norika was a sharp bark, but from a dog that was benign, at least for the present.

Mr Ikoshi and I left the party at the same time – he to dress for dinner at some high table or other, and I to escape the sight of Murdoch, who had been asking him questions about the *bushido* code, kamikazes and *hara-kiri*. There was a heavy drizzle, and it was natural that I should share Mr Ikoshi's umbrella as far as his hotel, which lay on my way. As we walked I found he was taller than I had thought, for his stockiness offset his height. I apologized for Murdoch, and Mr Ikoshi laughed. 'Of course, those are the things Westerners always ask about.'

'They hardly seem the most important aspect of Japan.' I wanted to sound urbanely tolerant, but with a sharp eye for essentials.

'Hai! But those things are especiarry Japanese. *Seppuku* – that is how we now say *hara-kiri* – is onry Japanese, and hard for others to understand.' We walked a few paces in silence through the rain, then Mr Ikoshi continued, 'If a Japanese is disgraced he can save his respect by this means. It is the same if the disgrace is his own or if it comes to him from another – especiarry if it is from his master.'

'So if a Japanese person – '

'Of course, *seppuku* is onry for men. A woman might hang herself. If she is ravished she would try to kirr the offender – perhaps while he is resting afterwards. Otherwise her famiry would try to kirr them both.'

We had reached the corner of his hotel, but he continued to talk, standing with the rain, which was now falling quite heavily, drumming on the umbrella and dripping on our shoulders. 'It is about honour and saving respect. Rike in some parts of Europe where they have the brud feud. There are many resembrances between the Japanese and the Itarians; both are fine engineers, both are fine artists, and both have a strong sense of honour.'

I said I thought the Italians were rather more flexible about it, nowadays.

'Perhaps. The Japanese also are frexible, but for them it is a matter of strategy. The tree bends in the wind, and so it overcomes the wind.'

We shook hands gravely in the rain, and I ran the rest of the way home in sodden shoes.

*

That night I dreamt I was woken by a scream, coming from somewhere near the bike sheds. Pulling on a dressing-gown, I stumbled down the stairs and through our short-cut passage to where the sheds faced the college wall. I didn't question that it was my business to investigate, or find it remarkable that no one else seemed to have been roused. Under the wall, my feet slipped in something that was dark and faintly sticky, and a drop landed on me from above. When I looked up I saw something bulky on top of the wall. I found I had a torch in my hand, and when I shone it upwards it lit Murdoch's face, horribly contorted and with blood dripping from its mouth. His body was jammed between the top of the wall and the row of rotatable spikes; they were turned the wrong way, and their cast-iron arms had been driven through him. In my dream the sight was firmly associated with an image of Mr Ikoshi, gravely nodding at the sight of the spikes.

Then, with the convenient encapsulation of dreams, I found myself dressed and coming to Norika's room in what was now daylight. Her door was ajar. I pushed it open, with my head lowered in fear, and saw her bare feet dangling. The note on the dressing-table read, 'The flower in a strange land mistakes the blow-fly for a bee.' By then I was awake, and I suppose the corny japonnaiserie must have been mine.

Obviously Mr Ikoshi's conversation had made a deeper impression than I realized, and my fears were increased by the fact that, apart from a burst of febrile cheerfulness during her father's visit, Norika had been pale and withdrawn since our 'talk' in the Cadena. When Murdoch mentioned at breakfast that on Friday the two of them were motoring to the theatre at

Gents, and then turned his eyes instead to Bernadette's chest, staring through half-closed eyelids.

'Tart,' he said again.

Bernadette didn't appear to have heard him. Josie and George and she were all watching the pot-bellied man; a smile on each of their faces, the same smile mirrored all around the pub. She was wearing her black sweater. Jamie looked at her hard. She was wearing no bra.

The man was still dancing. He was slopping beer onto the floor, elbows raised and glass held in one hand, seemingly oblivious to the departure of the girl. Oblivious too of Tom Mullen standing before him, staring down without expression.

He came to when Jacky returned the jukebox to its previous volume, calling almost at once for a whisky for Tom Mullen and staggering up to collect it. Tom Mullen remained where he was. Straight-backed, with his arms held rigid to his sides, he waited until the drink was delivered, taking it without acknowledgement and then turning sharply around to return to his place at the edge of the bar.

'What a tart,' said Jamie.

George looked at him. He said, 'Who, Tom Mullen?'

'Nah, his girl,' Jamie replied.

George shook his head, lighting up a cigarette. He flicked the spent match towards Jamie. 'Nah, she's just an exhibitionist,' he said. He smiled. His teeth were brown or else missing. Jamie stared at the tie trailing from his jacket pocket.

'Nah, she's a tart,' he said. But no one replied.

He lifted his glass and stared at Tom Mullen.

'That basta' Mullen hasnae bought a drink all night,' he said.

In a far corner a man with no shirt stood on a chair, bursting the balloons overhead with a cigarette.

*

When Jamie had arrived by cab from The Pig they were already well settled. George had brought with him his girl Josie, and she had brought Bernadette. Jamie hadn't minded. He was going to offer Bernie a drink at The Pig. He had waited until closing, but he hadn't seen her. He bought a drink for the whole crowd before he left. He had the money.

The Mount stood on a bare hill at the edge of the town, well back from the road, with the town to its front and the works to its rear. Before the Closure it had been where the men gathered before nightshift, overlapping at half ten with the men from the backshift. In winter the wind slammed the door shut behind you when you came in, and the toilets flooded.

Redundancy hadn't brought any loss in custom. The payments had been large and the pub continued to fill every evening. Unworked for, the money flowed more freely and the men began to arrive with their women. They came by taxi; left when it suited them. There were no last orders. Jamie liked it.

It was a long low-ceilinged room, packed tight round the edges with crowded trestles and chairs, the walls unadorned, in need of a repaint. The bar curved in a semicircle from one of the corners, a large alcove to its right giving onto a pool table and the toilets, a smaller alcove to the left housing the jukebox. In a display case over the jukebox a grey squirrel sat perched on a beercan, draped in blue tinsel. A few streamers had been hung over the bar, and balloons attached to the ceiling.

It was the balloons that Jamie had noticed first when he came in, misshapen and colourless. Then he'd recognized Bernadette and the others. He had gone over and sat at their table and they'd been talking about Pringle. He was going to mention the balloons but then he wanted to know what it was about Pringle.

'There's a load of johnnies on the ceiling,' he said.

'So what,' said Bernadette.

'There is. Have a look,' he said.

'How about getting a round in, Jamie,' said George.

Bernadette had tilted her head back, emptying her glass.

'Same again,' George said.

'And me,' said Josie.

Jamie hadn't minded getting the drinks in. He was of slim build and pushed his way easily up through the ranks to the bar. A slim build was always an asset getting served. His height could let him down coming back. As he was barely over five foot, the other drinkers often didn't see him, and spillages were always a danger. With two pint glasses in his hands he had eased his way through with great care, making a passage by calling out names as he went. It was useful to know and be known. It wasn't very often that he lost any.

'Not a drop spilt,' he said when he got to their table.

Bernadette and Josie were laughing at something George was saying. George had his arm slung across Josie's shoulders, the sleeves of his jacket rolled up to the elbow, revealing a tattoo on his forearm the same as on Josie's.

Jamie had swung round precariously to face the bar again. He felt unsure on his feet. There were two more to fetch, his and Bernadette's. She had asked for a whisky and he'd ordered a double, with a pint for himself. They were gone when he got to the bar.

Tom Mullen's girl was sitting on a stool beside him. She was listening to an old man with no teeth. He was leaning forwards with his face thrusting up towards hers. She was laughing, holding a double in her hand. The old man had worked with her father. Tom Mullen stood beside her, two full pints at his side. He wiped the froth from his moustache.

Jamie had ordered again.

He strained to focus on the clutch of notes and coins in his hand.

'How much again, Jacky?' he called.

'Two sixty, son, *two* sixty.'

'Aye, two sixty.' He fumbled with the money, letting a coin drop to the floor. 'Jeez, there's no getting a grip on the pennies at all,' he said. 'Here, Jacky,' he held his hand across the bar, tipping the money into the barman's hand, 'you sort it. Keep it. Happy Christmas.'

Jacky's wife had glanced at him as she pulled on the beer pump, and Jamie looked over at Tom Mullen.

'Who needs the hassle, eh, Tom?' he shouted. 'Plenty more where that came from, anyway!'

Tom Mullen had looked at him, eyes impassive beneath black eyebrows.

They were still talking about Pringle when Jamie got back.

He placed Bernadette's glass in front of her and curled his hand backwards, palm facing her. 'A double,' he said. She didn't look up. He slumped more heavily into his seat than he meant to.

They had all laughed suddenly then, tipping their heads backwards. George had finished his story. He wiped the back of his hand across his lips and reached for his glass.

'That's how ah heard it anyway,' he said. 'Cheers, Jamie.'

Jamie had waited until Bernadette lifted her glass. 'It's a double,' he said.

*

Jamie watched Tom Mullen's girl come out from the toilets. She was dressed and she had her hair back up. She brushed down the lapels of her jacket and walked quickly to her stool at the bar, sitting down heavily and unclasping her bag for her cigarettes. Jacky lifted a glass from under the bar and placed it before her. She drank from it immediately, saying nothing. Jacky spoke to Tom Mullen, who smiled.

'What's with the bogs anyway?' said Jamie.

'What's this?' said George.

'The bogs.' Jamie nodded towards them.

George looked over, and shrugged. 'Some joker's switched the signs about. The Women's is the Men's now.'

Josie leaned around George to face Jamie. 'There's nae difference,' she said. 'Ye can use either wan. Disnae matter.'

Jamie began to laugh. 'Nae difference! News to me, that! First ah've heard of it!' He laughed harshly, staring at Bernadette. 'Eh, Bernie!'

Bernadette uncrossed her legs, crossed them the other way. 'What?' she said.

'Nae difference!' He laughed.

'Probably,' she said.

Jamie looked at her earrings, he could feel his eyes blurring. He tried to think what she meant. It wasn't the right answer. Finally he laughed and flicked a beermat into the air with his finger, catching it on the way down. He tried again and fumbled.

99

A loud cheer rose up from a group close by. They began clapping their hands to a rhythm as an elderly couple got onto their feet to dance. The woman lifted one side of her skirt, holding her other hand aloft; the man wobbled his belly in front of her, red-faced and puffing. Jamie watched them. They looked stupid.

'Shall ah call Pringle over?' George said suddenly.

'Why?' said Josie.

'Shall ah?' said George, looking at Jamie and then Bernadette. He unhooked his arm from Josie's shoulders, calling loudly through his hands.

'Ho, Adam!' he yelled. 'Adam! Come here!'

He waved him over with his arm.

Pringle was standing by the pool table, watching the game. He held his glass close to his stomach, taking small sips, drawing on a cigarette. He looked over and seemed uncertain, and then he began walking.

'All right?' he said as he approached.

'Aye. Aye,' said George. 'Yourself? Ah hear ye've been away. That right?'

Pringle nodded, dropping his cigarette beneath his foot. Jamie felt in his jacket pocket for his Embassy's, passing one over to Bernadette. 'Thanks,' she said.

'Spain and that,' said George. 'We wis over there as well, me and Josie. Didnae see you anyplace.'

Pringle looked from George to Josie, and then back to George. He raised his glass slowly to the height of his chin. 'When did you go?' he said. He sipped at his drink.

'Got back a fortnight yesterday,' said George. 'That right, Josie?'

'Yes,' said Josie. She crossed her arms over her stomach, leaning back. She puffed her cheeks out and watched the dancers.

'Oh aye,' said Pringle. 'Be about the same time.'

'Where'd ye go?' asked George.

'Here and there. No one place.'

'Aye? Camping like?'

Pringle looked at his shoes, and looked up. 'No,' he said. 'Different hotels.'

'Hotels? Aye? Splashing out like?'

Pringle shrugged. 'Aye,' he said.

'Ah hear ye went wi' Sylvie McCloud,' said George.

'Aye. Ah did.'

'Havenae seen her aboot these days. She all right?'

Pringle took a breath. 'Aye,' he said.

'Did ye have a good holiday anyway, Adam?' said George.

'It wis okay.' He glanced at Josie. 'How about youse?' he asked.

George smiled and drew himself upright. He placed his glass on the table and reached an arm around Josie. 'Well, Adam,' he began, 'let's put it this way: Ah brought her back again. Ah brought her back!'

Jamie laughed, and Bernadette smiled. Pringle smiled uneasily too, pushing a hand deep into his pocket. He looked over his shoulder at the bar.

'Adam, Ah hear they've dubbed you Sealink now!' shouted Jamie. He winked at George. Josie was twisting to free herself from George's arm.

'You can fuck off, Jamie,' said Pringle. 'It's not very often Ah see you with a woman.' He glanced at Bernadette.

Jamie raised his arms above his head, rocking them from side to side. He began to sing. 'I am sailing, I am sailing, far away-ee, far away ...'

The song was taken up by some of the other drinkers sitting along the walls, glad to hear the sing-song beginning. Jamie raised his voice louder, almost shouting, aware that he was suddenly very drunk, that Bernadette was staring at him. Pringle edged his way back towards the pool table.

'For fuck's sake, Jamie, give it a rest,' said Bernadette.

He punched his fists into the air and laughed. 'Sealink Pringle!' he shouted. He let his hands drop heavily onto the seat.

Josie looked at George. 'You're a cruel basta', you really are,' she said. 'Just look at him. He's not got a friend in the world.'

'Aye he has,' shouted Jamie. 'They're all away on free holidays tae the Costa del Sol. It's his aine fault. He's a mug. Always wis.'

He picked up his cigarette from the ashtray, drawing deeply. The smoke smarted his eyes. He looked at Bernadette.

'So what's the crack then, Bernie!' he shouted. He needed a piss badly.

*

A bell rang at the bar. 'Last orders please!' Jacky was shouting.

There was no rush to buy drinks, instead a loud chorus of cheering and whistling. The elderly couple had got back onto their feet, joined then by another. The barman raised the volume on the jukebox to its loudest, and Bernadette stood up. She walked across to the toilets without saying a word.

Jamie slipped deeper into his seat, sliding his legs beneath the table. He watched Bernadette's backside until it disappeared through the door of the Gents. The inflated condoms overhead were jostling and shuddering in the blare of the speakers, and George was shouting something into Josie's ear. She was smiling. Jamie reached into his jacket pocket and drew out his cigarettes. There was just the one left.

When he stood up it was like stepping off a roundabout. He felt giddy, his legs seemed to pull the wrong way. He felt for his jacket buttons, and swayed backwards into the seat. He kept his eye on the toilets. He began walking, reaching for arms and shoulders as he went, past Pringle, past Tom Mullen and his girl. The door was lighter than he remembered it, crashing against the wall as he tumbled in. He stood where he was, allowing the door to swing back behind him.

'Bern!' he shouted. 'Ho, Bernie!'

Urinals, cubicles, water all over the floor. The light was too bright.

'Bernie!'

She was standing in front of him. One of his feet stepped backwards, stepped forwards again. 'Bernie,' he said, quieter.

'Jamie,' she said.

'Listen. Ah've been thinking like. Like you need a holiday.'

He put his hand up suddenly to stifle any objection. Her expression hadn't changed, she said nothing, stood still. 'No, no,' he said. 'Listen. You and me. It wasn't so bad, was it?' He peered at her, glanced at her earrings. 'Was it, Bernie? Hey!' She looked back steadily. She looked to his hair, at his chin, his nose and ears. He reached into his inside pocket, wrenched a wad of notes free. 'Ah'd no short. You can see that.' He stuffed the wad suddenly back again. 'Bernie, what d'ye say? You and me. Spain or someplace, disnae matter. Be like before?'

She stared at him, motionless, expressionless. Jamie couldn't be sure if he was moving himself, he reached out an arm, touching her breast. He felt calm. He reached forwards another arm, looking at his hands, one to the other. He spoke to his hands. 'Eh, Bern. Spain? How about that?'

Bernadette looked down at his hands, then back to his face. 'Busty Bernie!' he shouted suddenly. There was silence.

Bernadette took his wrists between her forefingers and thumbs, lifting them gently away and letting them fall.

'Fuck off Jamie.' She walked past him, and out.

Jamie glanced over his shoulder some moments later. The palms of his hands were tingling and they felt warm. 'Stoaters,' he said to himself. He reached into his pocket again, gripping the notes. He shook his arms from his jacket, wriggling his shoulders until it fell into the wash on the floor. 'Tart,' he said, kicking off his shoes, first one, into the wall, then the other, he had to kick twice, into the other wall. He put the money into his back trouser pocket and reached for his zip, slopping through the water to the urinals.

The door swung open behind him, slammed shut. A woman laughed, a man coughed at his side and began whistling.

'Needed that one by Christ,' he said. 'Bit of room for the next anyway, eh, son?'

Jamie looked at him, he couldn't think if he knew him. 'Aye,' he said. 'That's right enough.'

'You're enjoying yoursel', son?' the man asked.

'Aye,' said Jamie. 'Aye. Yourself?'

'Oh aye. Not often Ah don't. Cheerful Charlie, that's me.' He laughed.

The woman laughed also, inside her cubicle. 'Don't listen to it, son,' she shouted. 'He's a miserable basta' the rest of the year.'

'Nae thanks tae you, that's fer sure,' he called back. 'Happy Christmas, son,' he said to Jamie. 'Look after yoursel'.'

'And you,' said Jamie. He picked up his shoes. Spat on the floor. 'Leave the jacket,' he thought.

He opened the door.

GEORGES MINH

Jackson Webb

Bud Drain was big with a head like a bullet, thumbs in his pockets, white stomach drooping. Polly Daniels gave a party and he locked the door – it must have been the sewing room where she put my hand inside her sweater. Rob Vossi, Pete Hodges, Al Probasco, we swam at Sportland and cruised around that Denver April, lawn mowers chasing fat brown squirrels along the street to Pizza Heaven. Some hoods from Saint Regis knocked Bud down and burned his hat in Shoparama. We shook a lady's fire escape until she tossed her slopwater on us, went to Fun City, did all the booths and the roller coaster. Weekends, we took buses a lot and fired matchshooters, ideal in crowds with pins on the sticks, or biked down the parkway to Lowry Air Base, climbed inside the atom bombers. When Sundays hadn't much to do, I went to Georges Minh's.

*

The Minhs were new in Western Circle. They had rented the top of the Drains' garage and made the vacant lot a garden. They brought two sheep that lived in a crate, and their poodle yapped from a chain on the clothesline.

Georges had come to school in March. He was three years older but couldn't speak English, though he understood if you talked to him friendly. Miss Glosser taught me some French over noontimes and asked me to help him along.

He was dark and his face was Chinese. He wore blue shorts every day of the week and white cotton socks turned over twice. One day, somebody buzzed off his hair. He carried a satchel from his school in Vietnam, but it only had oranges inside and a jack-knife. I didn't know they spoke French over there.

Behind his apartment were steep wooden stairs to a porch with canvas chairs and a mattress. The first time I went, he smiled from the window, his round brown head too large for his body. The kitchen was shuttered-up damp – peas, carrots, beets on the table; a garden basket, chains of garlic. He had to make a soup of these before his mother let him out. I saw a rabbit running about, nibbling long loaves of bread tied with string. There was cheese in a cloth dripping into a pan, no bulbs in the lights, but candleholders. They didn't seem to have any rugs yet. Over the sink was a golden cross.

Mrs Minh wore furry red slippers. She had jade earrings and straight black hair. *'Ton nom?'* She patted my cheek when she found me exploring.

'Jack,' I said. I was tall for my age.

Her perfumed bathrobe said Yokahama and had a leaping tiger on it. *'Va aider Georges.'*

I helped Georges, but here too, the job was beyond him. He'd already spent the morning at it. I thought of better things to do than dicing onions, but Georges just shrugged and moved his hands.

After a while, his mother backed in, scrubbing the pink-checked lino on kneepads. I watched her legs and the sprouts of her bottom. Georges peeled marrows and never looked up. She sent me out to pick from the garden. Parsley grew beside the flowers, twists of iris, maroon tulip tops, lettuce and peastalks bobbing in clusters. I opened the leaves: a purple cabbage. *'Vite, pour la salade!'*

Georges was still busy after I finished. I rode around the field with the poodle, mountainside, circleside, schoolside, Polly. I rode ten minutes but he didn't come out.

*

We went to the stockshow and the railway station, Sante Fe Del Rio Norde. Derby, Fort Morgan, Brush, Cheyenne – AMTRAK Silver Flyer Service. From the brakeman's shack a hundred yards down, we crossed to the western platform: Salida, Grand Junction, Mexican Hat, changing Ogden for San Francisco. We hung on boxcars to Speer Viaduct and

E. Gomez Diversified Book Shop. Pete swapped the covers while I'd bullshit the guy and we took away *Teen-sex*, not *Robinson Crusoe*, heading back with fries and malts, and we tossed it all in a parkway bin, Hodges dragging last of course.

*

Muggy afternoons in class, high jets flying and the far rush of traffic. I thought, 'What does Georges know instead of this?' Whatever it was could only be better. He used to draw across his pages: temples, bridges, hillside towns. I watched his square-nailed fingers sketching. It seemed to be no effort for him.

Were they all like Georges where he came from? I got a library picture atlas. Vietnam was by the ocean, facing us: bamboo rivers, geese on the roads – flat country mostly, good for biking. China was there just beside it, south if you wanted a coral atoll. Imagine, places where *you* were the stranger, having choices, heading deeper. That was the beginning of it.

Georges Minh. Or whoever he was. Miss Glosser pronounced his name correctly, but the playground jeet went on and on. Red Rover, send over George's Minh. Or Dick's or Harry's. Georges looked back from the space of himself, as if we were making a movie about us.

He liked to fool around and wrestle, taking my notebooks, raiding my lunchbox. What he did never fitted his face or the moment. You could be in the middle of saying something and all at once he'd pin you down, his grey eyes smiling but not his mouth. I pulled my shirt right and called him an asshole, but in suddenness he always won. He threw an orange and it hit Bud Drain, broke on his head with a juicy splatter. Even the wall clocks held the hour, but Georges only grinned, his arm still cocked. Did it matter what followed that perfect shot? This was the difference of him.

*

At home, I spent most time in my room. The patio roof I also preferred because you could spy and no one would see you. The maple tree was fine as well, up in the leaves beside my window,

Mable in cleaning, the sun on the bookshelves. These seemed to be the only places where I didn't feel the sickness.

I used to be dizzy. They said, 'You're not smiling.' At Bauer's Restaurant or The Golden Slipper, wearing slacks, a padded jacket and tie, I felt alone and worried. During the Daniels' barbecues, playing ball or roasting weenies, I'd think how good it would be to smash things. Over the hedges, along the walks: miles of blocks and years of sameness. You could run all night and not get out.

I had stereo earphone Panasonic TV, Hit-Captain, Laser Wars, Turkish Harem – Paint-a-Number, Space Tennis, Combat Zone. I kept markers in books and magazines and typed at my desk behind a jap shade, memos, files of daily stuff, paper clips, tape deck, microscope, camera.

Georges and the poodle came over one Sunday. We took some cokes and pie upstairs. He tried the Rolling Stones on the headset, then we looked at our blood with 40× power. He leafed through *Playboy*, *Life* and *Time*, played Grapple, Stinger and Battle Line, but Georges couldn't seem to make any sense of it. He moved around and stood at the window, while TV gunships sprayed the jungle. We waded in the fish pool, shot a few baskets and after a while he went away, though Mother said he could stay for supper. It was May and the maple tree shaded the lawn.

'Gosh, he hasn't much to say.'

'Georges is from Vietnam.'

'Well, he's not much like you, Jack.'

School finished and we drove to our mountain cabin. Black and white magpies flew over the fields. Pale green alfalfa lay back like an ocean, then above the sandstone cliffs at Lyons snow came down between the pines. I fished from the boulders in Big Thompson River and tundra-hiked to Chasm Lake. Nights, you could see your way in the starlight. I followed the aspens along Wind Creek and found a hut with its chinked logs fallen. I walked there every day in July, sat on a bench by the lonely doorway, heard the beavers munching bark. The stream flowed faster, silent again – a brown bear threaded through the stumps, then just a lowly porcupine, his bulby sock-nose and sharp sides swaying. I wanted to stay until autumn that year, but my father's firm was building a dam, so we had to go to Denver sooner.

*

It was smoggy-hot on Western Circle. Mable had come the week before, dusted the rooms and turned on the Kool-Air. My desk was ready with pens and fresh blotters, but it seemed so dumb to be inside and have a city birthday three weeks before school. Bud Drain had a motorscooter, called me, 'Hey, shithead,' and pelted down the street. Al Probasco was still in Hawaii. Rob Vossi had gone to the Scout Jamboree. Sleeping late helped, and typing the journal, but I started feeling bad again. Mother said to phone Polly Daniels. I rode to Shoparama and Potts Junior High between the bike racks to the football field through a gap in the fence up their flagpole drive along the parkway and then instead of going nuts I steered to Georges Minh's.

Now they had a table and a striped umbrella, deep in the cabbage at the end of the garden. A thin-tyred bicycle was propped on the gate with strings in the grass to the chewing sheep. A man was there drinking a glass of wine. Some gold lace panties blew on the line, a black brassière and a T-shirt: *Tahiti!*

'I'm Eugene, how y' doing?' the guy said in English. In fact, he could have been from here, baseball cap, jeans and sneakers, blue mirror-glasses, snake tattoo. Mrs Minh hugged him and kissed his hair, but Eugene just looked like a big GI.

Georges came out in an ironed shirt. His arms had grown or his legs or something. His mother wouldn't let him change, so we went to the movies like that, triple-feature horror bill, then the shock of neon signs on the mall and greasers dancing in Pizza Heaven.

Next day, I showed him the Air Force Base. We rode up a ramp to the sentry boxes, Georges saluting, speeding through, even the poodle paddling past. Beyond the hangers: the wide reach of bombers. We climbed in the first one and tried the tail guns, visored helmet Stratofortress Vietcong attack. The flak was bursting all around when we saw the tiny streets and oil tanks, office buildings, asking for it.

'Okay, Captain, take controls.'

'*Kill them! Kill them!*' Did Georges say that?

A light went on and something ticking, warming up. We ran down the tarmac to the bikes far away but my feet wouldn't work because I was laughing and he was the same, crimped tight in his clothes, floating through the marvellous total moment.

We lost the dog and Mrs Minh cried. But Eugene bought another, a brown-spot puppy that dug up the onions. Eugene said Georges could go where he wanted.

*

Pete Hodges stole a whisky bottle and we drank it one afternoon in his basement, rain on the gutters, furnace gas roaring. The stuff was *fast* but I got outside when he cocked a pistol, silly bastard loosed a shot but I escaped the dizzy sick.

*

Georges Minh. His name appeared in the air like a wish. Strange, there was only this before: my punishment-room until the weekend, righteous Mable cleaning up.

Saturday, we made for Derby and Watkins. It was cloudy when we started, then red thunderheads folded on over the mountains. Locusts sang from the prairie grass. Wind dried our shirts as we pedalled along. Colorado State 10 crossed a stream and stopped, Larkspur County Borderline. We had extra tubes and a water canteen. A buzzard dived over the tumbleweed track, jackrabbits kicked behind the sagebrush. I enjoyed our quiet journeys out. We made someone stronger than either of us. Words didn't seem to mean a thing – they really kept you away from action, reminding you what you were doing. Broader days, undeclared, about the way they were for Georges. Once, we got to Rocky Ford and my father had to fetch us, drinking coffees at the Spur Café.

Georges liked matchshooters a lot, smoky trails streaking over his shoulder while he whistled along, gazing ahead. Then I'd swoop in, duck under the bar and put two close hits into the leaf pile, high, where the coloured tips were driest. One blaze was so large, it brought a fire engine. The stack was by some wooden boxes that crackled up and caught a trellis, then soon the shed was burning brightly.

Afterwards, we'd go to Georges' place, Eugene rolling cigs, the sky in his glasses, Mrs Minh glad with the radio on. She wore a bikini, polka-dotted, and now a little silver watch. I had never seen her look so pretty, slow eyes darker, shining red lips.

*

Mother's bridge group was once a month. To me, this seemed to be every week. All things had to polish and shine, each tea table and Venetian blind, doorknobs, mailbox, hall figurines. I put on a tie, carried drinks on a tray. Mable came early: 'Ain't *you* the slick chick!' I went around, met the ladies and took their smeared cups. And what did they say to me, serving ugly, yellow street leaves spinning down?

*

I took Georges to Fun City and out dirtballing. It was always twilight in the parkway spruces. Hours changed and I didn't care. Our lobs went out through breaks in the branches, firing blind except for the spotter, thirty feet up in the blue spiky limbs. Misses were a far-off spatter but the hits were terrific, like head-on wrecks, only the screech of brakes was later. Then came the crazy flights between tree trunks, palming them, counting them till the mouth of the Circle, where you had to be clear of the shouting behind and the bad mistake you'd thrown yourself into.

One time, some Mexicans ran alongside, not the harder way they were supposed to, caught Georges in the open and pulled him down. He fought for a while and called Eugene, but they grabbed his arms and kicked his face. I was the lookout and stayed in the tree. What good could I do? Georges was older than me.

The broken nose he got that day, scars on his meeting brows and chin, the gash from the slopwater lady's whole bucket – was I the only one who knew what happened to him? Slouched on the handlebars, thick legs pumping, beaked racing cap, or diving at Sportland in his jockstrap swim suit: how was it, being Georges?

Polly Daniels joined us on roller skates. We stopped on the corner as she glided up backwards, rose bandanna top-piece, white mini-skirt, I nearly regretted my still-mountain summer. We spread a blanket beneath her hedge, her mother off shopping, nobody present. I kissed her, then – nothing else developed. Maybe that was why she let me, even now with Georges looking on, flipping a jack-knife into the grass. He sat so calmly, it was almost expected when he lay beside her after me. He stood out from a black bunch of hair, stock, apart, and all disappeared with Polly groaning. I had never seen anything like it.

If you could do that when you were thirteen, then the rest of life would only improve. In a year or two, I wouldn't mind. But *then* his easy acts disturbed me. Would Georges forever be ahead, despite his awful luck?

Our families had a conference, and Reverend Lee Harvey came to advise us. Eugene didn't make it, only Mrs Minh. I was sorry that we had upset her, yet it wasn't what the Daniels said. Georges stared straight ahead, unbothered.

'But Jack, he's just a goof,' Mother told me, driving home.

'Why get involved?' My father's opinion.

*

Potts Junior High started that week, which covered up our troubles. Mrs Minh sent Georges to Saint Regis. I missed his company right away and even Polly's face was sad. We had said we'd get together on Sundays, go to the Air Base and the fire escape woman's. But I think that I had understood I would not know him long.

I had to be all sorts of people, do useless things and learn cautious facts. Georges was solid, he stayed himself without trying. Whatever the utcome, you found him the same. The morning we robbed the lockers at Sportland, he dropped our coins all over the place but didn't tell them who was with him. Our trips kept growing larger, too far, too good to make again.

I wrote about some we hadn't managed – how we hitched to the cabin, deep middle winter, and snow-shoed upstream with rifles and backpacks. Another time in California, we checked into a beach hotel, spray and breakers bounding in, rubber disco darkie lady. Georges' mother came as well and never mind about Eugene.

*

Bud Drain made the Wrestling Team. Pete Hodges joined the Pre-Law Club. Gus Schlobatka, Tex Stackpole, Scott Pandolfolos. We tried out for Track and Basketball. My mother had the Daniels over, and I went upstairs with Polly at once. I hugged her but she leaned and resisted, smiling though, still my friend! I just laughed at the narrow trudge of it, after Georges involved her.

There was homework and the days were shorter. The elms blew bare, then the window maple. That year, the Broncos went to the Super Bowl. My father's business was doing well. In October I became a poet. As detention, Miss Case made me copy a poem – the next afternoon, she told me to write some. She took the first, *Wind Creek Shack*, sent it away for a prize and it won. I wrote others, evenings, behind my screen. I left one unfinished, *Georges Minh*, because I never saw him again.

A Friday, late, I stopped by his house and walked across the snowy yard. The wooden stairs had lost their gate. Penning the sheep: the sun umbrella.

I called and his mother came to the porch with her long hair hanging down to her hands.

'Georges no here.'

'Oh. *Demain?*'

'*Demain, oui.*'

Why was she crying? I loved her.

Saturday, I couldn't go because the bridge women were arriving in cars. That afternoon, unknown to me, Georges stabbed Bud Drain in Pizza Heaven. There had been a wrestling match at Potts. Saint Regis lost and the teams crossed later. Rob Vossi told us how it happened; not exactly self-defence.

SCHWIMMBAD MITTERNACHTS

A Hollywood Adventure

Ronald Frame

I can make happen whatever I want to happen.

Tomorrow I'm having lunch at The Vineyard with Catherine Deneuve. I've decided so late in my long life that it's French beauty I admire most, and my good friend Catherine has deep-frozen it to perfection.

Three days ago I had lunch at Le Saint Germain with Paloma Picasso. We discussed CD, then our friend in common, Yves Saint Laurent. I told PP that I'd stayed with Yves briefly, at his elegant holiday home in Morocco they showed in *Town and Country*. We discussed elegance, Paloma and I, and I let her know how highly I reckoned it among the civilized virtues.

I've watched them pass through Hollywood, the elegant women of this half-century: Garbo, Greer, Ava, Nelly Nyad, Grace, Audrey, Claudia Cardinale, Anita Ekberg, Linda E. As I said to Catherine Deneuve in La Petite Chaya only the other day, after her *Today* spot, there is no true equality in this life, thank God; there *are* superior beings. I told her I was seeing Paloma P (Tuesday), and I said that superiority can be passed from generation to generation, and wasn't that a relief to know?

'I can make happen whatever I want to happen,' I tell my lady lunch friends, in all the best restaurants in Hollywood and Beverly Hills. They smile and tip their heads because they want to discover, they want to hear all about it.

Unfortunately I can't entertain here, on the premises (as it were), but that is no loss. People in our trade eat to be seen, and all my life I've dined out: cafés in Switzerland, fifty-cent diners on the Lower East or Fulton Street, and now – because there's an urgency about getting all the things in life attended to I want

114

to attend to – in the very best restaurants in north-west LA.

I tell my lunch ladies, oh what I could have done for you, the scripts you could have had from me! *You* would have read between the lines, seen all the affection I put into the character. As it is, you won't remember ...

They say they *do* (hand resting on my wrist), and I wonder. I haven't worked in the studios since 1954, and my TV work only gets shown now in the afternoons, when the shades are drawn and my girls are asleep in their rooms, in their satin lingerie: re-runs of sixties cowboy shows, and a fifties comedy series I once wrote with a team. These days it's camp, the series: it's called *Yodels in Yonkers*, about an Austrian family (Germans weren't thought 'publicly credible') who settle in New York City. Who remembers, who doesn't have the evidence of their eyes?

'Ah, *Yodels in Yonkers* ...'

Catherine's hand touches my wrist, she smiles. She smiles – that's enough.

But comedy wasn't my métier, I explain – even though someone did suggest me to the producers of *Hiram Holliday* and, later, *Get Smart!* Maybe I look too Teutonic to be convincing. I can make Carol Channing laugh when I call her up, and I think I can see my influence in Lily Tomlin's act. Long ago, before the war, Aryan was a swell thing to be in this place; later the studio bosses just didn't want to know you.

My mother was half a Jew, and I was born in Berne, but I had a name that sounded German and that was that. So maybe even my famous friends just pretend to have heard of me? What I'm lunching with is their *legend*, maybe: as people perhaps they don't exist. As a person perhaps *I* don't exist either?

I reckon I'm only worth my memories, and the offerings of my imagination. No one should be interested in how I live, where, what I eat when I'm not out lunching, what I eat just to survive, how I get my laundry done, how many pairs of slacks I have in my closet. That's too dull, it's nothing, it's beside the point. Anyway, who's ever one person? You go through this life, and the border of *your* personality, so-called, that's shifting all the time, like duneland; or you pick up habits and tricks, thoughts and opinions, from this friend, that acquaintance. People flow in and out of each other and sometimes you can't tell where 'I' stop and 'you' begin. That's fine, that's just how it should be.

Thank God.

I said it already – who wants to know how I fill the rest of my day when I've got my clean laundry back and I'm not lunching or calling from the pay-phone, to all my friends in the Hills, too many to tell you. I watch TV a lot, old films, those programmes, cowboy shows shot in four days. The cowboy actors were all gay, but you got used to that, and the queen acts between shots: all you see in Mr Reagan's America is the frontier spirit, and men with square jaws and flat stomachs, and grateful women.

I voted for Mr Reagan both times, but I never listen when the radio next door comes through the wall at me, all about Congress and those terrible gun-crazy places all over the world. I'm Old Hollywood, you see – I remember people telling me the great sign west of Griffith Park used to read 'HOLLYWOODLAND' Realty, until the 'LAND' fell off – I never stopped loving the stars, the unchangeable, women in the fullness of their grace, such beautiful women, born in heaven.

*

That's what *she* might have been.

It was in Switzerland, in Zurich, that our paths crossed first. I had an appointment at a fancy café to meet someone who knew someone in films, and *she* was at another table waiting to meet an agent who was working for another agent in New York City.

She was an actress, I recognized her. She called herself Sophie Niederhauser. I'd started out in the theater, and had a good memory for faces and names. She *looked* better than she acted. She looked great, *chic-kultiviert*; classy, as the English say. And some. And mysterious too, as if no one was going to get to know all there was to know about her – *if* there was so much, of course ...

That afternoon at The Glockenspiel she kept glancing over at me. Eventually she came across. She thought *I* was the man from the agency. I said, 'No.' She laughed, she was so embarrassed. A bit on edge, I guessed. She asked me my name and *I* was so nervous I told her my real name, not the one I was using to write under. Then I corrected myself. 'Peter Keller,' I said. It vaguely registered with her, I could see.

I stayed on in Zurich, just to have a chance to talk to her again. We met another day on the Bahnhofstrasse, by accident (more or less), and she told me she was being taken over to America. I still remember how she sounded, so excited and amused and incredulous and proud, breathless too. She said all her photographs had been sent out without her knowing anything about it, and they'd caught the eye of an agent who knew one of the senior European directors working in Hollywood. Gunther Volkhardt-Prinz, he was called. She was smiling right across her face as she gave me the name. I shook my head, meaning I was impressed.

'America's a world in itself,' she said. 'A whole world.'

I repeated her.

'They've got a Little Italy in New York,' she told me.

'There's a Chinatown too,' I said. 'Somewhere.'

'In California there's a place called Venice.' She laughed. 'With real gondolas.'

She was on a cloud, and when I took her for lunch afterwards she didn't seem to know where she was, or who she was with.

Later, though – at another place, in the City of the Angels, the New Palestine – *then*, I guess, she did remember.

*

Later was the next year, 1934.

A number of accidents – or colluding events, let's say – had taken me out to the West Coast. I found I had the same professional name as another German writer working for the movies, and somehow they confused our agents in New York. It was like a film plot when they told me, but by then it was too late: I was out there, it felt like no place on earth, and I'd decided I might as well stay.

Somewhere, in someone's office, I met the secretary to Gunther Volkhardt-Prinz. I'd heard his name a lot: he'd worked with some European actresses, turning them into stars. It must have been a difficult business for him, so I reckoned: they didn't have American temperaments, they didn't speak the language too well (if at all), they didn't like the heat.

I knew about the last film he'd made, called *The Sultana*. It had come out about thirteen or fourteen months before: it was his first, and very successful, vehicle for his newest protégée, a Danish version of Garbo. Through most of the movie she was in veils, which added to her allure. As the publicity posters put it, 'Who *is* Verena Karel?' In those days that was all you needed to do to pull people in: that, and using the sassy-sounding Continental name and those cool grey Skaggerak eyes peering over the yashmak. (People say we lived innocent and naïve lives then, but I wonder.)

The woman secretary was in her forties, tall, austere, European in the icy way Hollywood understood it. I introduced myself. At first she confused me for the other Peter Keller. Then, when I (politely) put her right, she was suddenly less interested. That is, until I mentioned another name, Sophie Niederhauser.

I watched her face set. Her mouth shrank to a straight line, her eyes bored into me. She shook her head. 'No,' she said, 'I've no idea who you're talking about.'

At the time I was working on a script from a short story called 'The Tired Old Detective', which the studios (the same studios that had Volkhardt-Prinz under contract) had bought rights on. The story was about a private investigator who's becoming over-sensitive because he's stale in his job, whose wife calls him a 'tired old detective' to his face, and who begins to suspect – with just how much justification? – that *she's* involved with another man in a plot to murder him for an insurance pay-out. Maybe I was too much influenced by that, and saw the world as my tired old detective might have done, over-reacting, reading too much into a situation. Or maybe not.

Any time in future I had to pass the secretary in a corridor, she pretended to pay me no attention: but I knew – I had gooseflesh – that she saw me very well, and she was keeping me close in her sights. Meanwhile I asked everyone I met about

Volkhardt-Prinz, and they gave me so many versions of him I didn't know what to believe.

On studio telephones I called New York late at night and rang round the film and theater agencies. I spoke to all those the studios had dealings with, but none of them could tell me anything about an actress called Sophie Niederhauser. One of them did have a record of a Swiss actress entering their books the year before, but her name was Maria Linsenmeyer: she'd subsequently gone out of circulation, and no one had been able – or had bothered – to trace her. 'That's the business, mister,' I was told.

I found the posters for *The Sultana* where they hadn't been covered over by others. They were starting to peel and tear. I stared at those grey eyes, and puzzled – I didn't know why I should be thinking it – remembering those other, azurine blue eyes I'd been looking into on the Bahnhofstrasse.

*

An automobile knocked me down when I was walking out of the studios one day, and I came to in hospital.

I was there for eleven weeks. Most of the time I could, I spent reading – whatever trash was going around. Next to me in the ward was a Polack who made riding boots for a living, a real craftsman. He told me the studio bosses and directors and the stars were his godsend: he didn't care where they'd all come from, if they'd crawled up from the gutter, now everyone belonged to Hollywood. 'Even you, young man, although you may not think it.' I shook my head. 'You'll never get away,' he said.

He told me about the legs he'd fitted, the beautiful calves. 'Not that they're all like that.' I asked if he'd ever made boots for Mr Volkhardt-Prinz. He nodded. 'And for Verena Karel,' he added. 'Funny thing, though: I went back, maybe nine months, a year ago, and her feet weren't the same. She told me they'd grown.'

'*Do* they grow?' I asked.

'Maybe she's a whole lot younger than anyone thinks.'

'She's got knowing eyes,' I said.

'I didn't see her eyes. She was wearing a hat with a little veil. Little, but long enough. In the house.'

'Volkhardt-Prinz's house?'

The man nodded.

'I heard,' he said, 'she's crazy about those looks of hers. She's scared they don't stay, they vanish. She's a real strange lady. Maybe flaky, like they say.'

*

Now people don't remember the name 'Verena Karel' when I mention it to them. Not Bette, not Doug. Sometimes I ask people in the deli, in Schwab's, in the street, no one knows. No one remembers.

Once she was going to be another Garbo.

*

After the accident I was left with a scar on my face.

An actor might have welcomed such an act of providence, but I didn't care for it, and I decided to have some minor plastic surgery done on my cheek. I'd just been paid for something I'd written seven or eight months before, and could afford to go into a clinic for a few days.

On the last day, as I was preparing to leave, I was standing at the window and (for some reason) I was thinking of Volkhardt-Prinz and his secretary when I noticed a car like the one the great man was driven around in making its way down the drive. Cadillacs were common enough in Hollywood, of course ...

Maybe, I convinced myself, it's something to do with the treatment: you're letting your imagination take over.

*

Maybe.

But I was like a moth to a flame. I searched out Volkhardt-Prinz's house, on Summit Drive. I used to watch the long black Cadillac drive in and out, and the blue Bugatti roadster with the open top. Volkhardt-Prinz always sat beside his handsome chauffeur. Twice I saw him with his arm resting along the back of the driver's seat and his hand on the boy's shoulder. The boy was young enough to be his son.

For weeks on end I'd been asking around about Verena Karel. I'd been told her address was a secret. The secretary had got to hear I was enquiring and had sent me a curt note: certain information was way off-limits. A couple of weeks later I had my accident with the automobile, and it was as I was lying in hospital that I wondered if Volkhardt-Prinz had her staying with him in the house. Then what the Polack bootmaker told me, about the fitting, seemed to confirm it.

When I came out, like I said, I spent a lot of time up on Summit Drive, near Breakaway House and Pickfair. There were high walls and dogs in the garden, and I didn't dare to go in. In the early hours, on the other side of midnight, lights would go on and off in the house. A few times I heard noises – shouts, screams. One night – or morning – when I'd stayed on, intrigued by the activity, the gates opened, and the Cadillac drove out. The blinds were drawn in the back, but as the car passed down the street a hand pulled one of the blinds back and a woman's face appeared. It was white, terrified. A hand clawed at the glass, till the blind was wrenched back into place.

The gates opened again. The Cadillac was followed by the blue Bugatti, being driven by a woman in a headsquare. For a moment I thought, the driver's face....

I didn't see them come back. I returned on the next few evenings, and walked round the walls and stationed myself in the shrubbery opposite. The dogs barked, but I heard no more sounds from the house.

*

Maybe half a dozen times, or more, I saw Verena Karel's photograph in the newspapers. She was always being escorted by Volkhardt-Prinz, his hand was always on her arm. She wore hats with veils, so you couldn't see her eyes, and coats with their collars turned up, even in the heat.

I discovered she was due to attend a gala première, and on the evening I joined the spectators outside the theater. I pushed forward to the front of the crowd. As she walked towards where I was standing, I called out something in German.

Not Danish – German.

Her head turned, she looked at me, seemed to hesitate. Then Volkhardt-Prinz tightened his grip on her arm, she shook. She reeled a little as he led her forward, guiding her steps.

A trick like that proved nothing, really – even the tired old detective would have realized. So, maybe she wasn't from Denmark; maybe hearing German distracted her only because it wasn't American English? It was possible she'd picked up some words from her famous German mentor, like shorthand code between them. But nonetheless I was compelled, drawn, to find out more.

*

It was difficult to learn more. Verena Karel's public appearances became rarer and rarer, and she never met her audience again at such close range.

But I persevered. I did: let that be said of me.

*

At the studio, production started – in great secrecy – on a new film starring Verena Karel. Entrance to the set was restricted, by Volkhardt-Prinz's express instructions, but I persuaded one of the extras (at a cost of twenty dollars) to let me take his place as a milling, muttering French peasant among what used to be called the 'atmosphere people' in the background.

On the set she was never let out of the sight of at least one of four persons: Volkhardt-Prinz, who was directing, the secretary, a white-coated woman nurse, and the uniformed chauffeur in riding boots. Around her was gathered an outer group: the costumier and his assistant, the hairdresser, the make-up hand, script supervisor, personal maid, a diction coach. They were constantly encouraging her. Dressed as Catherine de Medici and in smoked glasses ('Don't let the light hurt your eyes, *liebling*!'), she sat there, just nodding.

Once between takes I heard her raise her voice and declare petulantly, 'I'll do it if I wanna do it!' (The remark told me she'd picked up some American English, what she required; on the set, however – even as the high-living, libertine Catherine de Medici ruining sixteenth-century France – she spoke her lines with a decided Scandinavian inflection.)

In the course of time – that same afternoon – I was discovered to be an impostor, and instructed in no uncertain fashion to leave. I saw the secretary watching me as I was escorted from the building. Behind her stood the chauffeur, in pugilistic pose, eyeing me as if I had a face he didn't mean to forget.

*

I had an instinct I should lie low for a while.

I moved into new rooms. I started a novel, about a young Swiss playwright trying very hard to make it in Hollywood. I called my story 'Swimming Pool at Midnight' because I thought it sounded good: in fact, it sounds better in German, 'Schwimmbad Mitternachts', but the title never got used one way or the other, because the book never got published; it wasn't even finished.

I gave it up after a few weeks, and went back to scripting, for another studio on Melrose. I had a couple of breaks. I managed to put down half on a car. I rented an apartment out in Santa Monica, near the pier.

I hadn't forgotten Verena Karel – like a story I couldn't get right in my head, that eluded me, which I couldn't believe in enough to be able to focus on it properly. It struck me, it was better – safer – not to get involved anyway. A coward's way, okay, but Hollywood was filling up with cowards then, or at any rate with those who wanted to avoid having to make decisions of a moral sort: hence the German-Austrian influx, and all the hopeful young actors – Hollywood fodder – wanting other people to make decisions *for* them.

I heard from an old contact at the studios that the Catherine de Medici movie was in trouble, Verena Karel had been taken sick. At least, that was the official reason. My informer told me no one on the set felt they knew where they were with the star; one day she'd nod her head, do everything she was told, the next she could remember nothing, the third she was throwing a

tantrum and talking German so only the director could understand, the fourth she'd be as quiet as she could be, like she was
in a dream. '*You* work it out,' he said, 'if you can.'

*

Years afterwards, in 1947 (or 1948), I got word there was a
crazy lady in a private home up in San Luis Obispo, she kept
saying the name 'Verena Karel' and talking in a language no
one could make out.

I went to see her. After so long she was nothing like the face
on the poster for *The Sultana*, although she had the grey eyes.
She wasn't speaking, she just glared at me. To test her out, I
said another name, 'Sophie Niederhauser'. It meant nothing to
her. But I knew it wouldn't. By that stage of the story – with all
my tacky credits for lousy B-pictures no one remembered after
the last frame – I had the truth. If that word 'truth' ever meant
anything in this mixed-up, loopy, jigsaw land.

*

But back to then.

It spread like a bush fire round the studios where
Volkhardt-Prinz was shooting that no one knew where Verena
Karel was. He'd tried to discover himself, but when he couldn't
he'd had to bring in the police. They were saying he should
have told them earlier, they could have done more.

When I got back to my apartment one evening, I saw a black
Cadillac – *the* black Cadillac – parked outside. The chauffeur in
his maroon uniform and tan boots got out and we 'talked' –
which is one word for it. He said, very sweetly, he would give
me five hundred dollars for 'information'. A thousand dollars.
Two thousand.

Then the sweetness disappeared as he told me I'd get my
pretty face busted, split open, if they found proof I was involved
in it. Luckily for me a police siren started wailing on the next
block and he took that as his cue and climbed back into the
Cadillac.

I stood looking after it as it rolled down the road. Still a bit
dazed, I had the conceit to think that, if I'd been writing his

lines for him, I could have managed something more neatly turned, not sounding as if it had been memorized from a movie.

The car vanished. Like Scott Fitzgerald put it, night had come down on day like a curtain. (There are no moody, thoughtful twilights in this place.)

The road was empty. The police siren faded. I might only have imagined that it had happened: except that I smelled something in the heat of that dark evening, the trace of eau de cologne, fleeting evidence that – for all the conceivable arguments to the contrary – I hadn't been alone.

*

Soon after that I moved out of the apartment, and went down the coast, to faded Venice-by-the-Sea, to a place on Ocean Front Walk.

The ocean kept me awake, but I didn't mind insomnia. In the evenings, when I was working on a script, I used to come back from the studios, have a drink, and go out walking. Sometimes, under cover of darkness, I'd head for the Pavilion with its minarets, sometimes in the opposite direction, towards the ghostly ferris wheel or, beyond it, the Temple of Birth.

Sitting in a diner one night, looking out at a broken-backed gondola abandoned in one of the silting canals, I remembered she'd mentioned it to me – 'There's a Venice in California' – way back in Zurich, she'd said it on the Bahnhofstrasse.

Occasionally I'd feel uneasy, I'd feel there were movements among the shadows behind me. Once, I was sure, I was being tracked home, by headlights: not by a Cadillac or a Bugatti but by a taxi cab – I couldn't make sense of that.

Another night I came back and I knew someone had been in the living-room. There was no mess, nothing missing that I could see, but a box of paper clips lay scattered on the floor under the desk – and, at that period of my life, I was still famously Swiss in the cleanliness and order of my domestic habits. Then I opened the desk drawer and saw that the manuscript of the novel had gone.

I shook my head with disbelief: not at first for the novel's loss, but in total amazement for a motive. I started looking for clues, but simply (or not so simply) couldn't find any. And no after-trail of eau de cologne either.

Could it have been *his* doing, the chauffeur's? And somehow that accounted for his interest in me, because of the novel, what I might have written in it? But I'd told so few people about it. I tried to remember just who I *had* told.

Anyone who'd wanted into the apartment could have got in. I entered from an open balcony, and a kid could have twisted the lock. I had nothing to steal, the furniture wasn't mine, so I'd never thought about it, my 'security'.

*

The police called me in the middle of one of those hot, empty, dogday mornings when I was working – *trying* to work – in the apartment and feeling becalmed, tossed high and dry, by circumstances. They were sending a car to bring me down to Playa del Rey, they said, to the Alpenhorn Hotel.

It didn't seem I had the privilege to refuse.

The hotel was like any of those frail, spindly structures on stilts with flat roofs and balconies along that stretch of coast, erected from what seem to be common composite parts and put up on scrubby lots with no apparent thought for their future. What distinguished it (in a manner of speaking) were the name, and pine shutters at the windows perforated with the carved outlines of hearts, and a dusty Alpine horn hanging on one cracked plaster wall in the front hall.

And the owner, a diminutive Swiss Jew with a moustache and a yellow-and-white polka dot bow tie. He stood in the darkened lobby – the blinds had been lowered, because of the heat or out of respect – and (I'd been searching for years for the sight of someone doing such a thing) wringing his hands.

I was led outside by the officer in charge, out past a kidney-shaped pool. The heat made me think I must be in a witch's kitchen. I could smell tar from the roadway on the other side of the hotel building.

I looked about me, as my trade demands. Probably the hotel and pool weren't more than four or five years old; they'd been meant as material feats of bravery and optimism in the throes of the Depression. Already grass grew up between the chipped paving stones; paint had flaked from the rail by the pool steps and rust showed through. Dead flies specked the greasy surface of the water.

The body had been taken back upstairs to the bedroom, which had been signed for with the name Linsenmeyer. She'd been found dead in the pool, some time in the early hours of the morning: the time just after I'd got back for the three hours of sleep I seemed to be able to survive on now. She'd been lying face down, afloat on the surface. What did I know about it? they asked. 'Nothing,' I replied. 'Absolutely nothing.'

They showed me the manuscript of the novel, which had been discovered in the room. I shook my head.

They showed me the victim. I shook my head again. They lowered the sheet over the body.

It *was* her, I couldn't doubt it. They'd changed her nose a bit, it was a little shorter, bobbed. Her eyes were wide open, they wouldn't close: not grey like the Sultana's in the movie, but blue, the colour of a proper, bona fide Beverly Hills pool or – better – a Swiss lake, like the Zurichsee, on a fine-weather day. Her hair had been dyed fairer, to the Scandinavian, and the colour was coming out at the roots. But it *was* her: Sophie Niederhauser, a name and a face I still hadn't forgotten, however hard they'd tried to turn her into someone else.

I just stood shaking my head, and when they asked – very particularly – I told them I hadn't a clue who she was.

*

The questions went on for days. Elsewhere they were pumping out the corpse.

They found needle marks on her arms, and traces of tranquillizers, anti-depressants, sleeping tablets, boosters. Some people might have taken to the life better, I was told quite coolly and matter-of-factly, but it had all 'gone to her head'. That seemed to me the whole point, but I didn't say: the police on this job didn't look the most understanding in all of God's chosen land of manna, America.

'Accidental drowning' was the official verdict. I'm not sure they were caring much, until Volkhardt-Prinz showed up for the body. She was buried not as herself but as Verena Karel, in a fancy ceremony at Forest Lawn. One newspaper I read said Miss Karel drowned in sassier Malibu, in Paradise Cove, and nicely sidestepped the issue – that newspaper had studio interest in it – and some of the other press notices told different stories, although none of them matched. Volkhardt-Prinz or his advisers invented a myth that Verena Karel was such a star she liked to get anonymous occasionally and hide out. It seemed to confirm that she'd been destined to become too big even for Hollywood.

'She' died young, and so she was spared all that sweating and toiling having to prove it, that she was an extraordinary talent. But 'she' would never have survived; she didn't, so the possibility doesn't arise, and the notion's just an empty hypothesis.

*

I can't help thinking, naturally – what would she have been like as Sophie Niederhauser? Why did they want to turn her into Verena Karel? – but I try *not* to think about it. Then sometimes, when I least expect I will, I remember that face in the car as the blind was wrenched back, and the person I went to see years later in the Gethsemane Home for the mentally disturbed, and I tell myself, at least – twice – I saw the 'real' Verena Karel.

But was there ever such a person – one person – who was Verena Karel? Or, before the role fell to Sophie Niederhauser, maybe there were others? Verena Karels plural? In Hollywood does it even matter?

*

I had a funny feeling afterwards. It was as if, I thought, as if she'd been trying to become a character in my novel, my Sophie Niederhauser from Zurich. Certainly I'd left spaces for her, gaps in the story where she was free to come and go, if she wanted to.

Can it happen, an author comes to be haunted by his characters?

But I'm not a proper author, so how should I know, of what concern should it be to me anyway?

Volkhardt-Prinz was cleverer than any of us. He was the *auteur-directeur* par excellence, he had his own scenario written; he was only waiting, as the 'other' Verena Karel went into a sudden, unforeseen decline, spinning on her axis. From photographs he'd already cast the Swiss understudy, shortly before our chance encounter in Zurich, on the terrace of the Café Glockenspiel. To a man of his long experience in Hollywoodland we must have seemed like two orphaned innocents, hopelessly and helplessly adrift: about to be swept away beyond the reach of saving.

*

All the infinite possibilities in this adult, X-rated world – maybe the police really did think I was mixed up in it? – they could drive you crazy, clean out of your box.

*

When it came out I went to *Sunset Boulevard* five nights running.

I thought it was trying to tell the truth of my life but couldn't get it quite right, not quite. Something eluded it, got away every time.

After the movie I used to walk the streets a lot, Sunset, Macy, Alameda, Temple, long past midnight. I drank a lot of coffee to keep awake. Suddenly, somewhere in the LA night before dawn came in, still in the desert heat and glare of headlamps, under tousle-topped palms, on sodium-pale sidewalks, I would remember the bells ringing on the tramcars on the cobbled Bahnhofstrasse and the two of us standing talking, in the crowd, in the bright sunshine of day, our words flying from us and it didn't matter.

I've never really told the tale before, not properly, I've only hinted, suggested. The problem is, Catherine Deneuve is another generation. I've written to Audrey Hepburn, but her reply – and her reply to the letter I wrote after that – they must have got lost in the mail. Audrey has such tender eyes, so very *simpaticci*, it's like they're looking into your soul. They say

Barbara Streisand sometimes shows up to eat at L'Orangerie on North La Cienega Boulevard, but they also tell you her time's very taken up now she's a businesswoman: she's got the intelligence to understand, but maybe I'll make that a drink date, not lunch.

Did I say, on Tuesday it's Paloma Picasso and me, just the two of us, *tête à tête*.

OPTICS

Christine Adam

The small straight chair might always have been his. He felt the smooth support from elbow to wrist, and let his hands hang limply over the edge. He could almost have counted his own vertebrae, each one making contact with the cushioned back-rest. He accepted the posture the chair imposed with a mixture of wonder and fear, like a man who waits to be transported magically through time, or a man who waits for the pulse that will throw him into death. He knew that this last comparison was far-fetched, self-indulgent, though he had been gripped by a physical spasm when the woman entered.

The sharp edge of the optician's cuff scraped against his cheek as she slipped another lens into the cradle. Glass grated on metal, but her voice when she spoke was blurred, softly focused. She was wearing stilettos, and walked back and forth to the lit screen without allowing her heels to touch down on the vinyl floor. She flicked a switch and asked him what he saw.

He saw one half of a wheel, the spokes bristling with the urgency of clock hands pointing to every moment at once. The other half was merely a shadow, an after-image, which only faded in response to his attention. A muscle in his left thigh tensed involuntarily, relaxed, then again. To keep himself from analysing the implications of this, he made a banal calculation about force and mass, and reckoned that, if she chose, the optician could drive at least six hundred pounds into the lino. She was waiting. He described the semi-circle, and she added another lens without comment. Better, he said, feeling foolish.

Nothing was better, in fact. He had not improved. Things had deteriorated steadily since the first optician, a bald man in a dentist's coat, had repeated: But the *left* side, the *left* side – thinking, perhaps, that at twelve he still could not distinguish, or did not understand the terms. He had even gone so far as to tap his left shoulder as a clue. It had not made the spokes any clearer, but it had, at last, been scientific proof that something marked him off from the other boys in his class; that he was hopelessly, incurably different.

There had been everyday signs for some time. He had, for instance, always favoured the kind of glass marbles that were opaque – clouded with a creamy smear that the blues and greens tried to penetrate. No one else seemed to think them worth defending, and he won hundreds during the tournaments that came round every year, following the unwritten calendar that included conkers and kissing games. He spent hours polishing prize chestnuts against his grey shorts, and threading them on to strings with a darning needle. He thought his heart would crack every time he held one out for the slaughter. He also kissed girls who inspired other boys to opt for the 'Chinese burn' – a torture based on slowly twisting the skin of the forearm. Once or twice he chose it for show, but he had been worried and baffled for days, and finally thought it best to stick to kissing and jeers.

What the first optician had done was to supply him with a pair of very thick glasses, and the official formulation of a problem he had guessed at long before. He had not been surprised that one half of the test circle was blank, and from there it was not a major step to the conclusion that something ailed the right half of his brain – something that would prevent him from seeing half the world, or the other side of every issue. He had never consulted texts or asked any questions then or since; then, from ignorance and a conviction that the adult world was out of bounds; since, from fear, superstition, or both.

The optician drew a chair close to him and he tried to press his back further into the cushioned rest. He still vaguely expected Miller, the bespectacled, middle-aged man he usually saw, but all was quiet beyond the door, and it remained firmly closed. She clicked on a little torch and shone it into his myopia.

He regretted last night's seven pints in a way he would never have done if Miller had conducted the examination. He might even have been rather pleased if Miller had said: 'Your eyes are like a minefield, lad – fond of your pint, eh?' He could feel the tangled threads of ruptured veins, secondary roads to nowhere. He had stupid eyes – small, grey and unintelligent. Yet now this woman was staring at (*beyond*) his naked eyes. A heavy warmth spread upwards from the soles of his feet. He had jumped into a thick, bottomless pool and was drowning without a struggle. The oculist, young, fragrant and starched, probed the black holes of his mind, lighting their caverns with her little torch. If she found them hung with bats she did not seem concerned. He stared at the point of light with one eye, at her smudged, raspberry mouth with the other.

Martha's lips had been violet – the exact colour of little velvet ears on a toy lamb he'd had as a child – an intimate, yielding colour. He had often gone to sleep stroking his cheek gently with the velvet ears, but he had never kissed Martha. He met her long after kissing games had become private. She was twenty-one and, like himself, had won a year's scholarship to study German at Heidelberg University.

Things had begun badly for him. All the way from Antwerp it rained, and the sophisticated air-conditioning on the bus did not prevent his glasses from misting over, though the Belgians were apparently not troubled to the same extent. Nerves – self-generated steam. He felt threatened when an inspector simply asked to see his ticket. He had barely recovered from the shock of being unable to cope with his luggage: two suitcases, a sports grip, a shoulder bag and a small typewriter. In Victoria Station he left the typewriter standing by a barrier while he crammed the rest into three left-luggage lockers. He was disgusted to find it waiting calmly when he returned. It had not been stolen to spite him, just so that he would have to carry it all the way to the Black Forest. He had typed the letter to Martha on it.

The optician shifted her attention to his left eye. He blinked. The letter had not been an easy task. He started five times and wasted twenty sheets of paper. Only by the twelfth had he given in and typed on the backs of ruined sheets, admitting that this would not be the final version either. If he hadn't delivered it personally he would have wondered if she ever got it, and searched his desk-top a few days later, in case it should be lying there and he had mistakenly handed her a good-quality, empty envelope.

At the end-of-term party in May, the foreign contingent discovered that they had not learned in a full year the exact force of thrust required for a chorus of '*Ein Prosit*', and smashed several beer glasses at every attempt. The screams of the Manchester girl with the cut thumb were drowned by strains of '*Gemütlichkeit!*'. Martha leaned against a brute with perfect eyes, and moved her beautiful lips to say that his letter had lacked insight. The observation struck him as so apt that he shouted 'Yes!', in genuine response to clear critical thinking. In the morning he felt as if he had swallowed the glass shards that littered the table. The journey home was even more unmanageable.

The optician clicked off her torch, and tip-toed to the main light switch. He slipped his glasses on while her back was turned. She sat down again and made a few notes with an expensive-looking pen that had no pocket clip. A lady's pen. She slid it into her pocket nonetheless. Her left cheek was flushed in a charming, childish way. She looked into the corner for a moment, then said: Could he, perhaps, would he mind, did he have the time for her to run a few more tests ... She was doing a paper on certain phenomena ... if it was more convenient he could come back at some later date, or ... ?

He was a highly qualified, unemployed linguist. He had time. She indicated her watch uncertainly. It was almost five o'clock. No one was expecting him, he said, today or any other day.

He took his glasses off, folded the legs carefully and handed them over. Her smile was a little lopsided as she stowed them deftly beside her pen, and he noted with surprise that something had opened – expanded deep within, as if a mirror had been held at a most cunning, revealing slant.

WASHING THE BLANKETS

Maeve McDowall

Dull sullen rain varnishes the dark stone of the houses. Here and there a smooth-hewn surface throws back a glimmer of white, a sickening pale gleam. Two steps away, a stone gutter, clear water over the stones. Sea stones, a greenness, a pinkish light beneath the flow. Along past the byre, the old rowan tree, split trunk growing round a rock. A cat, wise for ever, eyes the emptiness of the house fronts. At the meeting stone, a rusty graip* lies where it fell.

*

There were two of them, with peaked bonnets, high above us on short-haired tall horses. They were not unexpected. Our old women, skeining new wool at their corner of the last house, saw them coming. And passed the word. Our elders mustered at the meeting stone across the path. They raised their men's voices, quick, discordant, talking through again what had been talked through before. Still hoping for agreement, for the finding of one voice.

But when they thought the horsemen would hear the lack of accord, they quietened. Then the talk was soft, between them and the newcomers. Hands were shaken. One of our mothers brought the drink and the ashwood cup. The cup passed from elder to elder, to newcomer and back to elder. And voices loudened, neighing brays of laughter jarred the evening. The old women, faces black and dead, stood at the corner. Watching the men, stranger and resident indistinguishable, lolling in the glow of evening.

The old eyes never left them. Our mothers, about the houses,

* *Graip*: a long-handled three- or four-pronged fork used in farming.

fed babies and ducks, milked cattle, saw to broth, spooned potatoes; sharp with us, hollow-eyed, hurried. As they always were. We were pulled in. But the noises at the stone went on into the night; the strange loud noises of men not at work; then the stumbling sound of the departing horses.

The elders, our fathers, shouldered no spades next day. The gathered, in twos and threes, along past our byre, under the rowan for its bit of peace. Away from the prying and scolding of the old women, working at their corner on the wool.

At twilight, the women spoke. Only the boys would walk out of the glen to school the next day. We were to go to wash the new blankets, over the Dun to where the brown-green waterfall tumbled down in whiteness to a whirling pool and vast slabs. Everybody knew the water near our byre was the best for drinking. The water beyond the Dun was the best for the washing of blankets.

Three of us were to go, three no longer small girls. We could milk, spin, wash, reluctantly as required. But the washing of the new blankets was something we had not been asked to help with before.

Girls and old women, picking out the track up the Dun. Two to each basket, the rolled dark blankets, cakes of hard soap, bread folded in a napkin.

The blankets we spread on the flat shelves of white stone and watch them wick up the peaty water. Soaping, squeezing, tramping. The old women stand back and sing for us while we work. We are proud not to be tired. We can soap and tramp for ever. The harder we tramp, the harder they sing. Until all the felted blankets are drying on the slabs.

*

They take off their own shawls and wash them, then their skirts and shifts. Their singing has stopped. We stare. Shrilly, they call to us. They are like the old skins that hang from the rafter hooks, their breasts like flaps of leather. Their bellies drag in white folds. They have frizzled hair below their bellies, and flesh hangs below that. We shrink and cower before these unknown bodies who walk now into the wide shallow water.

136

Wet, they touch our arms, slowly unfasten our clothes, throw them to the dry ground. Our narrow taut-skinned bodies never looked at before. They sit us each on a dry clean blanket. One puts her hand into the softness between my legs of which I never speak. She makes round movements with her fingers. I feel sharp pain. With her fingers, she marks my breasts. Another cups her hands in the water and scoops it down my front. Its coolness soothes. When I look up, the others too have a cross mark on their breasts, run over by pearls of water. The third asks a question: Do you know the horned pain? No, mother. Do not go with men once you know the horned pain. Fold your blanket and shawl it on you as a grown woman.

*

Walking back with the baskets, the air seems strange. A turf roof is smouldering. Our elders stand silent with our mothers. The horsemen are here. They are herding before them one of the elders with his wife, children, such belongings as they can carry on the broadest backs.

The old women move with fire. Down they go to the horses. They tear at the bridles, pull at the girthing, unseat the two men. They shrill and sing, hair flying, shawls tangling, legs and arms flailing with a young energy.

And now we three new-shawled women see something else that is new. The old women are on top of the two horsemen. They tear off their coats, snap off a collar, unbutton a brace, haul off white linen, bare their legs and ... can it be? We who have seen our mothers give the breast to babies, we who have seen our brothers make water from soft little snouts, we who have seen our fathers standing astride with their backs to us, we who until today have never seen grown bodies unclothed. A white duck's neck emerges from a dark weed bed. And there is another. And the old woman catch the ducknecks, then wring them two-handed. The men beneath squeal and roar and writhe.

The driven man has stopped in his progress to watch this, this pantomime of retribution. Wordlessly, he reaches for a graip from over his back. The third old woman motions the others to stand back. The bellies of the two men she strokes with long sharp tines of the graip. They lie in rigid silence, white from their unbearded faces to their twitching feet. She calls us near, the new-shawled women.

And still she strokes red stripes with the graip. We look down at these animals who think they own us. We look at one another. The old ones beckon and gesture. These men are yours, they say. Have them.

But we, who do not know the horned pain, we can only stare. As the house burns, the man and his chattels move on towards the shore. A little faster, perhaps.

*

They came for us all the next day. Every roof was fired. Our backs were all bent beneath the baskets and chairs, bottles and crocks. But it was new men this time, with their sticks and pitch buckets and strike-a-lights. Our elders were meek, our old women spent. The village was left to its cats, in the care of the cleft rowan. New women look back on the old life. The life of no horned pain.

LIFE SUPPORT

Guy Kennaway

Edinburgh. Easy Jack Plowright, the consultant anaesthetist at the Royal Infirmary, had not read the report fully. Staff Sister Coat, who actively disapproved of his handsomeness, stood erect in front of her desk and conducted the meeting at a briskness designed to annoy him. They discussed a patient called Helen Robertson; she had been admitted unconscious after a car crash six months earlier and still lay in an impenetrable coma.

'She is pregnant,' the Sister said crisply.

Jack pulled himself up from deep in a chair. 'Is she? Oh.'

'It's in the report.'

'I see. Well, that is, er . . . Do we know her husband?'

'He died. In the same unfortunate car accident.'

'Well, this does all look rather tragic, doesn't is?' Jack looked up at Sister Coat. He changed the mood. 'We'll need her scanned as soon as possible. Naturally, we'll operate and deliver the child by caesarian section. Ask Bob Morrison to pop in and have a chat to me about it sometime soon if he's got a spare moment, will you, Sister?'

'Certainly . . .' Sister Coat made a note upon her clipboard in her small tidy script. She then looked back at her superior, but said nothing. Jack began to feel that there was something in his Ward Sister's manner which was more than usually antagonistic; she had that air of dissent, or at least disapproval, and specific rather than general disapproval too, which made him anxious for her departure. But she remained, starched, in front of him.

He looked up. 'Is anything the matter?'

'Aye, Mr Plowright, I would say there is something the matter. Have you no' read the report properly?'

He had skimmed the report; he had read enough to know that the patient was in a stable, light coma.

'What is it? Do you think this pregnancy should be terminated?'

'Yes, I do,'

Jack thought he sensed in her opinion an obscene manifestation of her obsession with tidiness. He wondered whether she saw abortion as something simply neat.

'... Considering the extraordinary factors ...' she continued, 'it must be a duty of yours.'

Listening to her Scottish accent, he suddenly felt that it was his Southernness, his Englishness, that was provoking this.

'I know it's not usual for a girl in a coma to have a baby – but that's what's going to happen. So, please get in touch with Bob and inform the next of kin.'

The Sister moved towards the desk as Jack ran his hands through his greying hair. When she spoke, there was defiance in her words.

'I see no reason why I need inform next of kin. Surely it would be preferable to notify the father of the child?'

'The father died six months ago, Sister.'

'Mr Plowright, with respect, how do you reconcile that with the fact that the patient is only ten weeks pregnant?'

*

Patient Helen Robertson lay stretched out in peace under the dim blue glow of the night light. Around her bed worked support machines in the shadows; beneath her, like the deepest foot pedal of a cathedral organ, throbbed the hospital. Swing doors thudded shut onto long corridors, and the reverberating air conditioning thrust warm soft air into the lungs of the building. The patient's body rose and fell rhythmically; her eyelids, drawn thinly over her eyes, were motionless and smooth, as if her eyes, under them, were staring directly up at the cream ceiling. Connected to the hospital by a single slim transparent tube, she was like an organ in the body of that institution; a vital, unthinking, unconscious function, an integral part of the life of the place, a core to the mass, a heartbeat, a pulse.

On night duty again, Junior House Officer Henry Dyer stole barefoot down the corridor to check whether the student nurse sat at her desk at the far end of the vaulted ward. He watched her through the meshed glass of the fire door, her head bowed over a magazine, and then turned back towards Helen Robertson's room. There, he stared into the circular window set into her door.

She lies flat upon the unwrinkled bed, bathed in care, caged but calm, and her effect on Henry is like a wave washing over a shallow shore. His gaze still fixed upon her, he opens the door slowly and stands on the threshold. Her even breaths call out in the silence and the stillness beckons, like sleep to a tired, worn man. Deep in the room Henry pauses; it's warm here, the air thick with tranquillity. At her bedside he pulls back the folded white sheet and reaches for her slender, pale wrist, turning it in his hand to find the pulse. Touching the skin, he picks up her beat; steady, rippling thinly in her artery. Weeks ago, months ago now, he would have hurriedly flicked over his left wrist and studied his watch, but now he does not look at his watch. He does not want to time her pulse, he wants to feel it, so he closes his eyes and sits wearily on the bed beside her body. Soon, he raises her sinuous arm and rests her wrist against his face, where it soothes. Later he caresses her cheek, slipping his open palm easily on to her soft neck and shoulder. Outside, beyond, a long chime from a distant steeple rings in dull unechoed tones the hour of two o'clock. He turns and stares out towards the night, then turns back and lets the weight of his body fall gently on to hers, plunging his face into the laundried scent of the hospital pillow. His eyes open now, he sees her hair across the white in fevered close-up. There is a whirring, pitching silence.

*

At eight o'clock in the morning, after an exhausting night, Dr Henry Dyer left the Infirmary. He was expressionless as he stepped out on to the puddled tarmac of the car park where his sand-coloured Hillman waited; above him the sky had been broken up by a clouded dawn. Henry drove through the cobbled centre of Edinburgh towards Portobello.

On the map of Britain, the Firth of Forth is the crowing

mouth that bares its teeth at the North Sea. On the bottom lip is the suburb of Portobello. In the winter, when that wind blows cold off the sea, Portobello becomes a paperbag town with damp, littered beaches, but during the summer months, when the days stretch into the nights, and the Fife hills over the Firth shine green against the fresh blue, the seafront fills with people; young love parades itself in extravagant clinches, and old greying Edinburgh stands at the rails by the beaches watching children play with dogs on the sand.

Henry lived just out of sight of the sea; he shared a thin, modern house with a physiotherapist called Vic. This arrangement was unsatisfactory; they were distant by the standards set by even the most unsuitable housemates. She was a lank and untidy girl addicted to short cigarettes and cheap instant coffee. Henry did not like her smell and she hated his glazed silences, but they were thrown together by laziness and apathy; sometimes Vic decided to move out, to move further into town, but she always withdrew from telling Henry because she felt physically tired at the thought of dragging her possessions from her wardrobe and her bedroom floor and pulling them together for a move.

Driving through the traffic on the slope down to the seafront, Henry saw the beach rear up over the bonnet from between a row of bungalows. He swung left at the dirty pebbledash of the municipal baths into the slim artificial curve of the estate road, and was enveloped by the trim dull development where he lived.

With the car stationary, the handbrake pulled, and the engine silent, he winced at the thought of entering his house. Presently, he lifted himself from the driving seat and walked, cold and thin-shouldered, up the garden path of tarmac which was cut into the turf. He let himself in.

'Is that you?' caught him before he closed the door. 'Did you remember the cat litter?'

'Sorry, I forgot.' He clicked home the Yale and sniffed, then he bent down and picked a letter off the floor. It was a credit card statement. He turned it over and placed it on top of a highly varnished semi-circular table.

In the sitting room he crossed towards the kitchen door.

'There's no milk,' Vic said into her magazine.

He stopped, turned, and looked at her, watching her reach out her hand and feel for a packet of biscuits without looking up. He felt tired, and sad. Outside in the hall again, he saw the blur of Vic's cat on the frosted glass in the back door. Its paw scratched at the pane.

'Let her in, will you Henry?' Vic called. He went to the door, opened it, and watched the cat move limply, slowly away across the muddy lawn. He closed the door.

His mind was unclear; the coming day confused him in his tiredness. Upstairs his bed was unmade, but he fell upon it anyway, and pulled the blankets around his clothed body.

'Henry! Henry!' he heard through his door. 'Henry!' she shouted from below, 'is it okay if I borrow the car?' He did not reply. A little later he heard the front door shut with a slam and the engine of the Hillman start. Vic revved it long and hard, before slipping the burning clutch and pulling away, but he did not care. With her gone from the place he wavered on sleep. This is the time when his lives overlapped; when his memories of the night and Helen Robertson became seeds which grew up and clogged the gathering day.

In time, he pushed off his walking shoes with his toes. The shoes dropped, one, then the other, from the end of the bed on to the carpet.

*

At the Infirmary the operation to locate the man responsible for Helen Robertson's pregnancy was under way. Sister Coat was eager. She passed her duty roster to a ruffled Jack Plowright.

'Here is where we start,' she said.

'You don't think it's a member of staff, do you?'

'All I know is that it is a man. These men had access to the patient.'

'Am I under suspicion too, Sister?'

She ignored this remark. 'We can rule out the patients on the ward. None was capable.'

Plowright raised his eyebrows. He knew that his general

responsibility put him in the dock, but he was surprised to see Sister Coat standing up for the prosecution. 'There are other wards in the hospital.'

'Yes, there are, but although someone might have been able to enter the patient's room during the day without being noticed, it would be impossible by night. It is my responsibility to make sure that a nurse or student nurse is on duty throughout the night at the entrance to this wing. I am confident that this was the case. The man responsible must have been inside the wards already.'

'So you think it occurred at night?'

'Would you do it during the day?'

'I don't know. I didn't do it.'

This statement did not slow Sister Coat. 'It happened at night, and from the HCG levels and the scan, it was some time during the end of April or the beginning of May. There were no male nurses on night duty then. That leaves Dr Gillan, Dr Dyer, Dr Flaxman ...'

'... Hold on. Dr Flaxman, as you know, is a homosexual ...'

'I would hardly have thought that that would rule him out of our investigation. Raping a woman in a coma is not exactly conventional heterosexual behaviour. Or is it?'

'It isn't. Keep him on the list. Who else?'

'The junior and senior registrars.'

'Come on, not Eric, for God's sake ...'

'Unlikely, I will admit. ...'

'I'm glad you agree.'

'Because he was on holiday at the time. Which leaves only Dr Paston.'

Plowright lit a cigarette. 'Right. I'll talk to them all ...'

Sister Coat opened the window. 'And you'll be informing the police, no doubt?'

'Not yet, no. I'll be informing the Administrator. It is up to him to call in the police. Now, how is the patient?'

'The patient is pregnant, Mr Plowright,' Sister Coat intoned gently, adding, 'as a result of rape. I for one do not think that crimes should go unreported. After all, there are other folk at risk.'

'I'm only too well aware of the situation, thank you. You have been very quick to point out that you have done your duty; now please allow me to do mine in the way I think fit. How is the patient?'

In restrained terms the Sister reported on Helen Robertson. Jack closed his eyes.

*

In the pale bathroom of his house, Henry prepared himself for the night, rubbing away the sweat from the nylon sheets under the sharp fluorescent light. Before running the bath he scrubbed away the ring of dirt left by Vic, and removed from around the taps her uncapped bottles of shampoo and synthetic oils. Later he shaved with great care and ironed his shirt before dressing and going slowly down the stairs.

In the sitting-room Vic was listening to pop music on the radio.

'Hey, Henry, you wouldn't make a cuppa for me, would you?'

He boiled the kettle on the old hob, feeling wretched, longing for his lover and the deep night ahead.

'Do you mind bussing it?' she asked, as he laid her cup on a mat by her side. 'I've got Quincey Jones tickets; Glen and Ray said they'd come ...'

So later Henry pulled around his blue macintosh and wound his way through the housing estate to the bus stop. The wind had moved round to the south-west; above him the clouds were dark, but on the horizon the sun still shone strongly, silvering slates on the municipal buildings in the High Street, and making the falling rain white. This rain falls thick in the summer, like a heady northern monsoon, making the homes moist, the air damp and the women sweat in their overcoats as they drag their shopping homewards in trolleys. Henry stood on the pavement looking up; behind him, a rank of flags advertising some commercial concern stretched out rippling from their poles. Edinburgh is a city of flags; they don't tangle and knot there, they flare out against the distant backdrops: the Pentland Hills, the slopes of Fife, Arthur's Seat and the Castle. They are free up there, clipping the wind as it passes on by, high up above the people in the streets.

Always a conscientious Junior House Officer, Henry Dyer, in a white lab coat, with his concerned, serious expression that rarely left his face, set about his duties efficiently. After completing a ward round with the Staff Nurse, Sister Coat approached him.

'You'll have noticed, no doubt, that Helen Robertson has been put on four-hourly BP and monitoring,' she said, watching him.

He looked up, catching her eyes. 'Oh. Why's that?'

'Because she's pregnant.'

His first reaction was jealousy. He thought the child was the patient's husband's; he panicked, he did not think it through.

'She doesn't look pregnant to me. She's been here six months ...'

'You'll be surprised to hear that she is only ten weeks pregnant.'

'What?' Realizing now. 'It's not a delayed implantation?'

'Hardly.'

Checking every avenue: 'The coma may have slowed germination. It can.'

'Not in this case, Dr Dyer.'

'How do you know?'

'She was menstruating regularly when we admitted her.'

'I see.' He looked down at the floor.

Sister Coat was due to go off duty. She began to wrap a scarf around her head, and pulled a worsted coat from the hat stand. 'It's a sorry day for the Infirmary ...'

He watched her take from her tortoiseshell handbag a compact mirror; looking into it, she arranged her hair under the scarf and pursed her lips. 'I just pray to God,' she continued, 'that the animal responsible is caught as soon as possible. Think of the patient. Poor hen.' She turned, clicking her handbag shut. 'Good evening, Dr Dyer.'

Henry remained motionless, listening to her footfalls recede and her farewells diminish as she moved away through the wards. She left behind, hanging in the room, the scent of a sweet, chaste cologne. Alone, he was free to express his emotions. He leant back in the chair, brought both hands up in front of his face, then clenched them into tight fists, and shook them, with joy and triumph.

When night settled in the hospital, wrapping itself around the wards, when the glimmer of the weak yellow bulbs lay in pools on the linoleum, liquefying the metal of the furniture, when, from afar, across the Meadows in Marchmont, the Infirmary's windows winked shut as the rooms inside were darkened, then Henry passed once again in front of his reflection to enter patient Helen Robertson's room. He touched her arm, he laid his hand upon her shoulder, he leant his head close to hers, and he knew, immediately, that she knew she was going to have his child. Now he cries. Bringing his arms softly around her narrow back he brings her swiftly up towards him. His mouth open, he laughs in silence, shaking with pride, accomplishment, their love. There's too much inside him; he breathes out and holds her away from him, staring into her blank face, her closed eyes. He kisses her dumb mouth, trembling. He feels, without question, within her, deep dark longing for his life, stirring now and calling him over and over again. It is a silent landscape in there, but Henry Dyer, Henry Dyer is familiar with the place, treading gently, carefully, at first, easing himself into her quietude. And she, on her side, can sense his unalterable trust, his hope, and receives him there with utter wonderment. In this place they are the last two alive on earth; here they lie upon a pinnacle above the waves which wash and crash far below.

He breathes in gasps, lying against her; she remains staring upwards through closed eyelids; her breath now a sigh at every exhalation.

'Oh no,' he whispers, lips moving by her ear, 'no no no no, don't sigh ...'

But in her sighs are her fears; in her stillness the weight of the argument against them, which she can no longer keep from voicing. Isolated, they plunge awhile, falling in the terrors that flash below them in the dark: the terrors of separation, the terrors of that world apart, against which their defence of love is flimsy thin. But for just this one moment, at least, nothing can be said against them for just now they are wrapped up and sealed with one another in a different, possible world.

*

In the morning, Jack entered the Infirmary. Sister Coat was already there, waiting outside his office, wanting to tell him whom she thought was responsible for her patient's pregnancy.

'Ah! Sister Coat,' he smiled, 'morning!'

She looked up at the clock in the corridor. 'Good morning, Mr Plowright. May I talk to you for a moment?'

Jack wheeled to a halt at his door. 'Of course. What is it?'

'In private.'

'Certainly.' He turned the handle on the door and pushed it open to allow her to pass through first. Occasionally he amused himself like this with petty gallantries towards Sister Coat.

Standing still in Plowright's office was Dr Henry Dyer. When they saw him, both Plowright and Sister Coat stopped dead. Henry was dark-eyed and exhausted, but resolved. It was this resolution which made the consultant hesitate; he knew Henry to be a man who threatened no one, but around him now was a territory marked out in his glance.

'Dr Dyer.' Jack laid his macintosh slowly over the back of a chair, watching Henry all the time.

'I have come to tell you something.'

Plowright motioned Henry to sit down. Sister Coat smiled briefly and began to shut the door behind her.

'Sister, we'll talk later,' Plowright told her, not allowing her this scene.

She left them alone.

'It's you, isn't it?' said Jack, without emotion.

Henry appeared not to hear. He took a deep breath. 'I am resigning from the Infirmary. I am going to marry Helen Robertson. She is having my baby.'

Under pressure, Jack found himself joking, stupidly: 'For a moment there I thought it was going to be something important.' He was in difficulties. He stood up, walked around the desk. He paused, then, 'Henry, what the hell is going on?'

'I don't expect you to understand. We're in love.'

'You're in love?' Plowright leant his head towards him. 'You can't even talk to her.'

'We don't need to talk.' He held his hand up towards the consultant, anticipating an interruption, adding quietly now, 'We don't need to, you see ...'

'Henry ...'

'... We understand each other without that.'

Jack remained staring at him. 'All right. Tell me. I can see how you might think she's sexy. I mean, we all know she's bloody pretty,' here Henry closed his eyes, 'but what the hell induced you to screw her?'

There followed a long pause that turned Jack in on himself as he watched this man. Finally, Henry broke the silence.

'I didn't want to.'

'You didn't want to?'

'No. She made me. She wanted to. She said I had to.'

'She didn't say anything, Henry. She can't talk.'

'I know you can't understand. We can talk to each other. It's the truth.'

'How are you going to marry her?'

'I don't know.'

'Do you think she's going to come out of the coma?'

Henry looked out of the window on to the rooftops of the houses which jostled each other to the south. Beyond them, the Pentland Hills rose into the grey. He did not turn to Plowright when he spoke.

'She can come out of the coma, if she wants. She told me. She can come out, but she's scared to, I think. It is a big step ... for both of us, if she does ...'

With sympathy, Plowright asked Henry if he were mad.

Henry turned from the window, refocusing. 'No. I'm not mad. Can you believe that? I'm not. I don't know how all this is happening, but it is. I am not mad, that's the truth.'

*

Jack allowed Henry to leave the hospital. They shook hands in silence. Jack was sorry.

Henry walked through Edinburgh down to the old docks at Leith. He could not account for why he was there. Hands in pockets, standing amongst the newly converted warehouses, he watched a building being knocked to its knees on a distant quay. The noise of demolition came late, long after the first puffs of dust which clouded the air across the water. He stared passively at this world which meant nothing to him, upon which his senses had diminishing purchase.

*

At two o'clock in the afternoon Henry Dyer arrived home and was arrested by the police. Vic stood in the middle of the sitting-room wearing pink slippers and smoking a cigarette furiously. Her first reaction, when she heard the policeman's charge, was embarrassment. She wanted Henry out of the house, and this concurred with the wishes of the officers. A group of women gathered outside the house, drawn by the blue flashing light of the squad car. Henry looked straight at them as he was led across the black tarmac. He recognized none of them. A boy on the corner of the estate turned his head to watch Henry through the back window of the car as it drew away on to the main road. The boy had red hair.

The course of justice is slow; it moves forward amidst sheaves of written statements and calls of claims and counter-claims; it pulls behind statements for the defence and statements for the prosecution, it is delayed, it is postponed, but finally it achieves its own end.

Here is Henry alone on remand; here is Henry with clasped hands at a table staring at his fresh young advocate; here is Henry being led to court through an underground passage; here is Henry looking down at his feet as he stands in the dock. And here is the law. It is all confusion to him, but through his passive bewilderment he can see that something is going wrong. The fresh young advocate says nothing of the plea of love. Henry turns to look at his defender, but it is too late, the right moment has passed, there is nothing more that is admissible. Another man now talks amongst the rustling whisper of the courtroom. Patient Helen Robertson is now the pro-

secutor's. She is held up and twisted in his hand, she is unravel-
led coldly in persuasive border tones, she is wound up again,
she is packed away safely, she is going to be all right in the care
of the Procurator Fiscal. She is smiled at, she is pitied, she no
longer belongs to Henry. It all happens without him seeing her
again. She is in their hands now, and Henry walks silent, like a
condemned prophet, convicted of raping the girl who loves
him, and sentenced to imprisonment.

Naturally, the newspapers take an interest in the case. A
photograph of Henry, grabbed while he was being led away
from the dock, is passed among the press and blown up. Beside
it rage accusatory and damning headlines. Out of it stares a
scared, disarmed Henry, his eyebrows raised in wonder, his tie
a little askew, his gaze a hurt innocence, his mouth open and
questioning, asking, wordlessly: where is she now?

In prison the nature of his offence makes of him a social
outcast. He is silent, detached, isolated anyway, but none of the
prisoners makes any attempt to bring him forwards into their
lives. He stands in a gap in the queue for food, and then sits
alone to eat it in small, regular mouthfuls. Criminals at another
table watch him, point him out, and shout. Later, a group of
them turn on him and fell him to the tiled floor of the kitchen,
where he lies foetally while they kick his head and body.

Bruised, he lies like a corpse in a ten-foot isolation cell. For
six months he talks to no one, answers no questions and asks
none, even with his eyes.

In another cell, in the Royal Infirmary, Helen Robertson is
stretched out with fading pulses, dying. The months of his
absence have drawn blood from her face, have closed her down
for good. One night, on a floor beneath her in the hospital, the
staff in the operating theatre prepare for the delivery of her
child, which, on the condition that it be healthy, is to be
adopted by Sister Coat. Her short interview with the Adop-
tion board has convinced them that she is ideally suited to bring
up the baby.

At eleven thirty at night, draped, Helen is wheeled over the
linoleum floor by two uniformed porters. The silence of her
room kisses the squeaking trolley a goodbye. Exactly half an

hour later Mr Bob Morrison, the Consultant Obstetrician, watched by a moody, reflective Jack Plowright and an excited Sister Coat, lifts from the patient's abdomen the child. It is smacked harshly into this life, and its mother slips into death.

In prison Henry lies stretched out under the nicotined glow of the night bulb. At the very moment of Helen's death, he clenches his body in a spasm, arches his back, tendons leaping from his bones, and screams a deep, long yell, which echoes through the empty corridors of barred cells. His head is thrown back, his every joint white with the effort of calling out the end to his love.

ROUND THE SQUARE

Philip Hobsbaum

'... and haunt the places where their honour died ...'

The shadow of the Post Office falls black across the square. Soot-blackened warehouses, mostly disused, rise up and, in their turn, cast shadows. But there is light. The moon, like a yellow hole punched in the sky, illuminates the ugly statue at the centre of the square raising his arms to defend the children. Around him, railings rust, barring children from his paltry plot of green. And round and round the square, in ceaseless march and solemn circuit, go three men. They have nothing in common apart from their species and their love of one woman, now dead, who used them so. Heldar says:

I'm tough. I wouldn't have got to where I've got to if I wasn't tough. It wasn't done by soft soap, I can tell you, no, the iron fist in the iron glove, the harsh answer that provokes wrath, the knee in the balls, the shove against the loom, quick deal holding your liquor when the other party's half cut, knowing who to know and getting to know them quickly, being there half an hour before the other chap – it didn't come easy. But I won. I own four factories, one the biggest of its kind, a house on the top, a cottage in the Dales, a Chelsea flat, four cars, one for each direction, a wife, a girlfriend, four kids at college and grammar school – one of them a little swinger, you should see her knickers, wouldn't keep a pussy warm. And minis – I said to her once, I did, are you inside that dress getting out or outside that dress getting in! Oh, I've won, I've won, I'm good for five hundred thousand on the Wool Exchange or anything else that I care to sign my name to, but it didn't come easy. Where I came from there were punch-ups every night coming home from school, there were bad times on bread, potatoes, an egg if you were lucky, with the old man on the dole right through the

Depression, though things perked up later, still we never were much class. I took her home once, Boody Thrapple, the lass that made a hassle of my life, I took her home, but she said nowt. I will say the old lady made her as welcome as she could, put the fire on in the front room we'd used once for Dad's funeral, best china, nice little sandwiches, plenty of home-made cake, Alfred and his wife round, silent and embarrassed at big brother and his beautiful girl-friend from the sexy city, she kept quiet at home but she laughed all the way to the station – well, it must have struck her as funny, the terrace house, low ceiling, the electric log fire and artificial geraniums and three ducks flying up the wall to Laura Knight's ballet dancers, all done in the worst of taste, she said, and with so much effort – aye, it must have seemed a joke. But she didn't have to laugh. I said nowt, it didn't seem fitting, but I held it against her and she knew I held it against her. The journey back besplattered with bloody marys all the way was not the best I've had, though I took Boody everywhere. The worst trip was to London with her daft teenage daughter, Bert Weems' kid that was; well, what d'ye expect from Bert? Boutiques, discotheques, Carnaby Street, King's Road, National Theatre, *Clockwork Orange*, I tell you I took 'em everywhere – I found her no laughing matter, I can tell you, spending four hundred pounds in a week that sent me on the bottle. She could always, could Boody, create an atmosphere and she said that Quintin was lonely, poor lonely Quintin, ex-boy-friend, ex-colonies, ex-lawyer, ex-everything, so what did I do but ring him up and ask him to dinner, mainly, I must admit, to get a look at him, but also to keep her quiet. Well, he came all right, did Quintin, bumbling public school idiot, murmuring polite nothings and trying to get her hypno-tized until I asked him, straight out, now what are you going to do about Boody, her daughter, and, for that matter, me? He said he'd like to take her for a motoring holiday. A motoring holiday! It's the first time I've heard it called that. Oh no, lad, I told him, it's more than a holiday that Boody wants. She's got a lifestyle, she wants a big house and an icebox and a telly and a cabinet full of drinks and friends round half the night – where is your house, I said, son, and where are your friends from? He said he'd buy a house but said nothing about buying friends, and Boody said to him, what can you do for me, Quintin, and I thought what can she do for him, but bloody well said nowt, and all he would say was 'I love you, Boody, come with me, Boody, my love' and she got up and leaned over him before my eyes – would you believe it – she'd tarted herself up like the Pope's breakfast for the occasion, one of those long Indian skirts, red pattern, ratine, and a taffeta blouse, white taffeta, all virginal on top, aye she looked like a million dollars but she acted like a she-goat groping this chap, damn near, before my eyes. I'll tell you – there was on the sideboard of this flat an awful object, a great stone phallus twice the size of your prick – it came to me, I can't deny it, that I could brain them both, he had his back to me, the daft custard, and her – well, I'd have smashed her face with it and stuffed it up her gee – final gesture of contempt and disaffection. But I couldn't believe it, I couldn't believe she'd go with this bumbling idiot with his glasses and his accent – 'I can't help it,' she said, bending over me and I swear Boody was crying, 'I can't help myself.' Couldn't she, though? I know one thing, I could help braining them, and I still wish I'd done it, with him outside in the hall, shuffling, calling softly, 'Boody' – I couldn't believe it, but she went all the same and I could have cut my throat. Twenty years back I'd been packed in by Sheila, lame Sheila, pretty mill-hand, and I thought, well, lad, there's drink, and I drowned myself in bitter – it cost a bob or two but after a month I came back, and believe me, I was clean. So I thought, you daft ha'porth, you've more brains at forty than to kill yourself for a woman, aye, or swing for her either, so I punished a bottle of lovely Glenmorangie, demolished the Armagnac, glugged down the vodka, found myself at six in the morning talking to her dachshund through four bottles of spirit and a very bad head when the phone rang. It was her. Oh, what a humble whisper, saying could she come back. She could, aye, and did after two more bloody hours, stinking like a she-goat from that chap's bed. I'm ashamed to think of it, I cuddled her and kissed her and took her upstairs, passed out like a pig and then it was Tuesday. Well, I've had grief, punch-ups and frame-ups, friends sticking the knife in, smoked dog-ends from pub ash-trays, seen my old man die, really afraid of dying, I've been poor, now I'm rich, all done the hard way, slog, twist and slaughter – and I've had good times, gambling in Las Vegas, whoring in Managua, dancing nights in Cairo, skiing in Lausanne, surf-riding off Nassau, I've four cars, four cars, four children, a wife and a mistress, four factories, one of them the biggest of its kind, but always, all my life, I've remembered that moment, her, a real lady, in long Indian skirt, bending over me, looking down on me, real tears in real eyes and then following that idiot down those fucking stairs – yes, H. Hamilton Heldar, boss of Heldar's New Mill, cock of the Wool Exchange, master of men, Alderman, JP, worth half a million, cowered before that woman, and reached for the brandy with one hope only, that she'd choose to come back. I think the men know, I see it in their eyes sometimes, pity behind deference, contempt back of the pity, I've broken men in every sense for doing half what she did, I can't understand it, I'm not soft, I'm not a coward, I've done well, I tell you, from terrace to mansion, but for one more night with Boody, Boody gone from me, for one night with Boody, I'd give it all back!

*

Past Illingworths, the big drapers with the ugliest shop-girls in town, past Hoyle and Woofenden, the great furniture people, past the office of the Carders' Institute, black brick and gold lettering, past Eden Street with its banks and exchanges worth half of Yorkshire, past Muckbeck Street, a vista of decayed warehouses infecting the town like damaged teeth, a rat-stocked sewer seeping beneath, past the Regent Cinema showing Sins of the Flesh *and* Vampire Woman, *past the Great Northern Hotel where many a vast deal has been shaken hands over while the whisky warmed, past the railway station – every village past Shipley and Guisely through Burley-in-Wharfedale to Ilkley and Skipton – past the corner where Harry kissed Betty and the shop-doorway where Brian fingered Ken and the fountain where Alec was caught pissing but later released because his father was Councillor Bosomworth, Chairman of the Watch Commit-tee, and the jeweller's window which Drunk Ossie cracked with his skull while stooping to puke and did six months' time because his father wasn't*

*Councillor Bosomworth or if he was he wasn't admitting it – back again
to Illingworths the great drapers with lingerie so old-fashioned it's come
back in again, go three figures, one tall and upright, one soft and epicene,
one momentarily lost in the shadows. It is the epicene one that speaks:
Weems.*

... if it wasn't enough, Boody, forgive me, I did my best and
who can do more? Didn't I work for you, cut costs, save up, buy
a lovely house between Menston and Guisely, it meant I had a
mortgage and had to commute in – but still you had a garden
and a lovely view. It meant I slaved at the mill, you know how I
disliked it, accounting, invoicing, checking others' taxes – then
back to the little house we bought to be so happy in, to be told
about my manners, my appetite, my grossness – 'Sex means too
much to you, God we're in the red again, let's have another
drink, go out for the night' – out to the roadhouse, Harry, Ivor,
Gerry, back to our own house – 'Christ, I feel ill.' You could
stay in bed but I had a train to catch, shuttling to Heldar's
every mortal day while you were painting – you worked, I'll say
that for you – mountains, skyscapes, I'll say they were good –
that's how I stuck you, Boody, you and your pictures: I lived in
those pictures – sometimes was a cloud brooding over Allerton
sucked into chimneys, sometimes a slope naked and sunkissed –
you never kissed me as the sun did those meadows – sometimes
I was a peak, but often, too often, a high mountain lake where
you poured your sorrows, reflecting only the day's disgraces,
rain, mist, sunshine, troubled grey sky – 'You have lovely eyes,'
you said – seven years at Heldar's hid them with spectacles
bleared by all accounts back to a tacky floor, last night's carpet
stains, tinned food or bad food or no food at all, and the sketch
for a painting that took what breath I had away, showing a man
in bed all alone, listening to the radio flat on his back, looking at
the ceiling, eyes like grey lakes troubled by the wind, and
suggested, implied, never clearly stated, the suspicion of a
woman hovering in the shadows looking at him secretly with
pity and contempt. Then I had a dream – I'll never get over it –
I don't want to get over it – a dream that will last me the rest of
my life: I dreamt we made love, for once it was beautiful, I came

when you wanted me, you cried out 'Lovely', so glad to make you happy, my beautiful Boody, but I got up, was talking, you listened absently perched on the armchair you kept in our room, when suddenly I saw you stare past my shoulder with a look of welcome never there for me – I felt a terror I've never stopped feeling – turned round and saw a man huge, at ease, kindly, whose eyes rested on me in quiet compassion. I said, 'Boody, you sent for him' – she said, 'I couldn't tell you, I wanted you happy', and at that moment the bedroom blotted out: I saw a cathedral, great arches, stone columns, stained-glass windows framed by curtains, amber sun pouring in warm autumn day, the organ was pealing slow polychromatics, Messaien or Greenwood – but what you must remember is I was in the bedroom with Boody and that other, yet I couldn't see them or the room round them or hear them or call to them; only those great aisles lit with amber sunshine, the organ throbbing, the arches vaulted far above my head; and then indeed I knew what it was to be mad. I blundered from the bedroom – I couldn't see or hear it – through the door and hallway; all I saw was arches, aisles, pillars, windows, sunlight, heard the organ pealing, and as I staggered blindly through sights so irrelevant, bits of the vision peeled off, flaked away – I saw I was in the sitting-room and there was Boody stripping as though I wasn't present, changing her blouse – I said, 'Should I be here? Boody, do you want me?' She said, 'Bust off, buster, I know where to go.' I went back to the hallway through bits of the cathedral – I still could hear the organ, see patches of sunshine – and tried to use the phone, I needed a friend, but I couldn't read the figures and a Workman from nowhere said, 'Let's get the account straight ...' I awoke screaming, Boody thought me dying, I wish I had, that hour, for still, when not working, the cathedral comes back. I know that transistor, I know the bed neglected, I know the hell that starts at three in the morning when masturbation, mandrax, whisky won't numb it – so I obeyed the Workman and worked ever after harder and harder – Boody, of course, left, but the pain of that parting was nothing to the dreaming – through accounts, invoices I still hear the music, and one day, I know it, I'll be back in the cathedral, arches I can't touch, columns that dwarf me, sunlight that blinds me, organ that shames me – my friends can come canvassing, Harry, Gerry, Ivor, to bedroom, to hospital, they'll not find me there, I'll not see their gestures, careful, cheerful, social – I'll be among the arches, the columns, the curtains, the sunshine, the organ – they'll never find me there. And if that's not enough, Boody, forgive me, I gave all I could and who can do more ...

*

Round and round the square, and the moonlight for some reason enhances the bulk of the post office, magnificent heresy of Victorian gothic, obscuring the cathedral, really St Peter's parish church, crouching behind it, and the misery of North Wing and its immigrants and the white pride of the new flats going up beyond. A wool city! Built for it, made by it, full of monuments to the fleece from Heldar's New Model Mill stretching two miles up Listerhills Road down to the strands of weft or patches of fluff you find on your carpet or your spectacles. Everyone here has catarrh or asthma or a leaning towards the highest incidence of thrombosis in the United Kingdom as they haul themselves from the square up to the squalid heights of Bolton Woods or the commanding heights of Heaton which are normally ascended in a Jaguar or a Mercedes-Benz. Everywhere from the square radiates outwards through reminiscences of wool – the Woolcombers' Arms, the Fleece Tavern, the Lister Inn, you get it in the very names of the pubs. The library is overstocked with Phyllis Bentley and Thomas Armstrong and trouble at the mill, and there'll be even more trouble at the mill the next time Heldar blows his top with the dyers' union or the weavers or the woolcombers. One couldn't rage like that unless inside was a turmoil, a volcano, and the three figures continue their circuit round and round the city square, shadow walking into shadow, the moon looking down on them with cold pity and contempt and a touch of fear, this winter night, and then out of the shadow come these three men, with nothing in common save Boody, save beauty, their common need and inheritance, one big and commanding, one plump and careworn, and the third a faceless man, a man you'd see anywhere, a private detective, the next-but-one in a queue or a railway compartment, indescribably suited, waiting over a pint or a cup of coffee for another man who will never come to that pub or any café – but, inside, an endless labyrinth of caves, tunnels, falls of rock, ravines unexpectedly opening before your unsuspecting feet, stalactites growing downwards but never quite meeting and kissing the stalagmites rearing themselves higher and higher towards them, and you fearfully exploring with your fitful torch still darker precipices, deeper inroads, rusted workings propped up by rotting timber as though once, once, there had been an explosion so terrible that nobody could repair the machinery or shore up the roof about to collapse on your alarmed head – oh, you fly, through wandering tunnels, past falls of rock and cliffs of fall, stumbling, lumbering, hoping for the gleam of light at the end of some tunnel that will lead you to the open sky, leaving him to his subterranean world, Frank Greenwood, D.Mus., FRCO, organist and scholar, sometime composer, respected citizen of this town, who speaks, but only to himself.

It takes an artist to know an artist, I said, dear fellow-artist, friend, partner, lover, but I cannot trust you. Trust me, she said, trust me, trust me. Come, come, why don't you come? I told her I'd been beaten, rejected, defeated, and I'd set it all to music – you can hear it in my tone-poem, the screams of the dying, the rattle of the loom, slurp of blood on the floor, the uncertainty as to whether yard or gut is stretching, the pause after an unresolved discord that lasts, when I'm conducting, exactly a second longer than the audience can bear it – you can hear me there, I said, I will never again trust anything but my art, dear fellow-artist, I said, please settle for that. If you don't want to be lovers, we won't be lovers, we'll be friends, we'll be strangers – I'll settle for anything. But love me, she said, and by God, it was easy. I'll never forget our meeting, I saw her in the audience – too slim, I suppose, a wicked mocking mouth, quick bird-like turn of the head, and, when you got closer, sensual Italian eyes, a prying, mocking green. Don't try to get to know me, I told her, I'm underground, buried but intact, you can hear it in my music. 'But I want you,' she said, 'I'm not like other women, I know you've been hurt, I can hear it in the key-change, the fugue, the stretto, the pleading coda – but you have to love someone, you have to trust someone, you have to live with someone, let it be me – do you love me, dear lover, love me, love me, oh lover, come to me, come, come!' I gave myself to her like a mineshaft exploding, she screamed in my arms but

I was the victim – I even thought I would give my music, those intervals of suffering, those long-delayed cadences, that put-off resolution sliding from key to key into endless renewal – I'd give it all for the ultimate orgasm lasting the rest of both of our lives. I gave it, I gave it, the years we lived together, we laughed, we danced, we had agonies and crises but never a dull one – she'd laugh at me at dances, making friends of my friends and teaching them to laugh, too; I should have remembered she'd no friends of her own, those funny mocking eyes, that high clear voice, the light figure of a girl less than half her age – we were living in style on my personal appearances, TV shows, concerts, *régisseur* at festivals, anything but music – I had laid down my pen. Oh, but she painted from dawn until sunset, she painted the music I wanted to write – the springs I had thwarted, mountains I never scaled, the sunrise avoided, the pure sweet air – all that was missing from my Symphony of Weavers I found in her landscape, her endless lake of districts, her winds and her mists, sunshine and cloud, herself more evanescent, more changeable, less tangible than wind across the water or mist on the moor. The first three months were ecstasy, the next six fulfilment, the six after, let us call it mutual satisfaction, and six months after that we'd bouts that were frenetic when we, momentarily, got back to almost where we'd been – but the last six were torpor, the last three depression, I getting slower, drinking more, becoming dismal, and she, happy that my day was already finished, danced up to her studio, painted like an angel, then, come down, would look at me as though I was a thing with no right to be there or here or anywhere – and yet I couldn't lose her. Early in the morning her dressing was a ballet – bird-like turn of the head, pulling, snapping, turning, flexing limbs for comfort, still graceful, still dancing – if only I had written what inspired that dancing, you can see it in her pictures, mist, mountain, lake, the lake, the mountain – yes, see it in her painting done in my seed, the blood of my life. Who took her from me? Was it Heldar or Quintin? It doesn't much matter, it was she who flew off – you graceful bird at sunrise, dear Boody, dear Thrapple, you sought out my secret mine and then blew it up – and now quietly in my cave, pits of fall exploring, I work deeper and deeper to ultimate dark, while you, dearest Boody, flying into sunshine mock me with your clear voice, artist of the sky.

*

And round and round go the three shadows, not one thing in common except the human desire to be loved and their love of her who hurt them so. Past the huge Post Office and the little cathedral sheltering in its shade, past the great drapers and the great furniture store, past the misery of North Wing and the unfinished elegance of White Towers, the gold lettering shining out from black institutes, the disused warehouses and the banks and the Wool Exchange and the streets stumbling upward, ever upward, to the squalor of Bolton Woods and the solicitors' paradise of Heaton Park, dominated by the already greying newness of Heldar's Hill which absorbs its own filth but not that of its neighbours, round and round they go, past the horror-show of cinema and the nevergo of the slatternly station and the vertigo of the great hotel where only the biggest brokers send out their bills in an ever-flowing tide of Scotch and soda, past the corner where Betty fell, and Ken, and Ossie, and Heldar and Bert Weems and Dr Frank Greenwood who therefore haunt the rounds of the square of their common boyhood with its ugly blackened buildings and grotesque statue at the centre, failing to be guarded by its failing palings from the insults of the children whom it failed to protect from scrawling and scratching their way through lives disfigured by failure, broken by betrayal, smashed as surely as bodies under a fall of rock in a mining disaster, yet living it over and over again. And enjoying it, moreover, again, enjoying it, enjoying it.

SUNDAY

Astrid Wilson

Going to church is like going to the theatre for her, she has to get dressed up. A bright blue coat. A hat. Pearls. A big black handbag.

Barrie, she always says to me, Barrie have I got too much lipstick on?

No I say.

Look properly, she says, look properly. Really *think*.

So I stare at her. Thick lipstick is completely wrong, I think, but of course I don't like to say that, so I stare at her and after a bit I always say no, no, it's not too much, it's just right.

Bed of roses, she says, bed of roses, that's the name. A soft pink, I suppose you would call it. Wouldn't you?

A soft pink, I say, looking at it on her lips. Yes, it's a soft pink. It suits you.

This makes her happy and she says does it, does it really, do you really think it suits me? And she looks at herself in the mirror, posing. Posing for a man.

She is always happy before she goes to Mass on Sunday. She sits at the dressing-table and puts on her make-up. She puts heavy powder on her nose. She puts on eyeshadow and mascara.

Well, she says, you may as well make an effort, don't you think? You may as well make an effort for the Lord.

She walks slowly into the church and people smile at her and say hullo. She does not kneel down because she cannot kneel down. There is always a fuss about her stick.

Mass begins and I listen to the voices like the sound of the sea and I look above the altar at the faces of the angels painted gold. They are like God, I think, that is what God looks like.

Dear God, I say, help me. Please let me do well at arithmetic.

163

Please help my mother. Please make her whole.

I listen to the priest when he reads the Bible. It puts me into a kind of dream. I grow peaceful and feel I am a part of the world. I like all the people sitting around me. I feel warm and not lonely.

God looks after you, the priest says, God looks after his own. We must do his will. We must not shirk from it. He sees our efforts and rewards us. We must trust him and give him our hearts. He gave us his son. He wants us to give him our hearts.

Yes I say yes yes yes.

*

Then we get home and she is always angry. She is always angry about the lunch.

I knew it, she says, I knew it. I knew it would come out like this. All fatty. I thought I told you. I thought I told you not to get a fatty piece. *Veined* with fat, I said, *veined* with fat. I thought I told you. I knew it would be like this. I knew it the moment I saw it.

I did try, I say, I did look. I asked the butcher. A good piece of meat, I said, for my mother. You know what she likes.

You're lying, Barrie, you're lying. You don't care. You just don't care. You've never cared.

It's not that bad, I say. Look at this bit. I'll give you this bit. It's all right, really. Why don't you try it?

She picks at it but after a bit she says, I can't eat it. I can't eat this. She pushes her plate away.

I eat mine and then I have some pudding. Then we go into the sitting-room. She sits in a big chair and begins to talk.

Oh, it was all different when I was young, she says, it was all different. I don't know what's happened to the world. We had so little but we were happy. I want I want that's all you hear today.

We were grateful, she says, we were grateful for what we had. We didn't have much but we didn't complain. We didn't go for holidays, we went for day trips. We went for picnics on the Pentlands.

The flowers, the flowers we found, it was marvellous. Ragged robin, meadowsweet, forget-me-nots. Marsh marigolds, dark yellow, growing in the water. Oh, I remember it so well. I remember lying on the grass and looking at the sky and listening to the larks. I didn't have a care in the world.

I didn't have a care in the world, I didn't know what was in store for me. She stares at the fireplace.

Then she begins to talk about men. They are selfish. They don't care. They want the good things in life, they don't want to know about the rest.

I don't want you to be like that, she says. I want you to be different. Her voice goes soft. She looks at me. She touches my arm. I want *my* son to be different.

I stare at the plants on the window sill.

TAKE-OVER

Naomi Mitchison

As a European I could not, of course, take part in the revolutionary movement of the late twentieth century, but it was well known how my sympathies lay. In fact the revolutionary council did me the honour of asking my opinion from time to time, even occasionally taking my advice. Certainly I was able to help a little over their external image and to counter some of the straight lies that were being spread. They sent me back twice to put their case in Europe and America; I believe I had some success.

It was impossible for anyone other than the medical team to go into the city itself until the epidemic had worn itself out. The team had the most modern type of protection against the terrible infection risks, but even so there were a couple of deaths in the early months. Gradually it became less virulent. At last, after rather more than two years, we were allowed back. The first clearing of the ruins and what had been left in them had been done by para-military units, again in protective clothing, but there were no casualties, so now it was thought safe for civilians such as myself, though outsiders and in particular the press and television representatives were not yet allowed in. One photographer had disguised himself and sneaked in but had been caught and would probably have been shot but for the intervention of a few of us who talked the Committee out of it, explaining how badly this would be thought of in other parts of the world.

When we actually went in some of us felt some anxiety, though we were assured that it was quite safe. My own anxiety was not for something as trivial as my own health, but for what I would find in a certain place. I had managed to make sure that this was where I would be sent. We started from the camp and then had to make our way through the smaller streets which had not yet been cleared; we had been instructed not to shoot rats or small animals. They could be dealt with later. But it was possible that larger predators might have been attracted, probably jackals or wild dogs of some kind. Someone had said there had been a tiger viewed, but that was probably an invention. All I noticed myself were the squirrels and once a harmless snake. We separated at what had been the monument and I looked up at the hotel; for a moment the upper part seemed unchanged, the rows of windows softly dazzling. Well, we would see. It was quite simple to walk up the steps and through the swing doors.

My companion had been a kitchen worker. It was quite usual for young Arts graduates like Salim to take such jobs, which usually meant becoming politicized. He had some hair-raising stories about kitchen bribery and what often happened about the stores. I think he had also helped in the elimination of some senior but much disliked bosses. But that, after all, was two years ago. Since then he had been working as a literacy teacher. A nice chap and knew his way round the hotel, especially the lower-ground-floor complexes. I gathered he'd had a girlfriend in the cosmetics and hairdressing section; but she seemed to have disappeared. He only mentioned her with a kind of sideways casualness.

The last time I had been to the hotel myself was just before Christmas two and a half years ago. There had been great bowls of white orchids with genuine imported holly through them, as well as a decorated Christmas tree, a real imported Douglas spruce. In Australia we always made do with a young casuarina. There had been other bowls of orchids everywhere, and real gold orchid brooches and bangles in the showcases. Yes, it had been like that. And a fountain with lilies in bud and blossom and yet more orchids. Easy enough to see where that fountain had been: there was dried scum in the basin. And there were the long counters and the notices still up.

Behind the counters it had been all elegance, warm welcoming by trained staff and, for that matter, efficiency. The girls all spoke English as prettily as they dressed. You changed your money, you picked up your letters or your key; it had all been so smooth. I went to the back of the counter with my torch and took a bunch of keys. There were papers lying, files snapped in place, a desk computer no doubt untouched all this time, even money: worthless stuff. I had to grope for the keys; even with a torch it was darkish behind the counter and somehow I felt awkward. I came away with as many as I could carry as well as the one I specially wanted. I looked about. Something unpleasant had happened to the carpet and of course with no lights one was liable to trip. The ground-floor windows had never been important and now they were blocked with greenery, mostly the bougainvilleas and alamandas which had ramped away instead of staying neat little bushes in tubs.

Salim had been downstairs. He came up with an armful of tins. They would be all right, he thought. Naturally everything in the freezers had gone; if you opened one the smell would knock you down. As for the cellars, there had been special orders, which we obeyed. They were no temptation for Salim, but would have been for me if things had been different. They used to have some really marvellous hocks. I remembered them. And there was no reason why they should not survive perfectly. 'But you must see the vegetable kitchen,' Salim said. 'Cucumbers, beans, pumpkins, peppers, many, many seeds and those little plants, how they got back on us when the wet got in! Everywhere! I could make a meal straight away: you know there are fruits burst, there are mango and pawpaw seedlings, little oranges and a grenadilla climbed out of the grating. Even the rice sprouted! Ah, but that needed sun, it shrivelled away. But oh, you must see – wherever light came in.' He was laughing a lot; it was nice having something to laugh about.

It surprised me a little to see how quickly the plants had taken over the ground floor of the hotel. After all, it had been in the middle of town. But there had been a piece of formal garden at the back, well looked after, and beyond it on another piece of land a few big trees which had made a pleasant background for the big swimming pool and the terrace. And in front there had been a row of tubs, begonias, lilies and so on. And there had been two monsoons between then and now.

When the front windows were broken, whether by storms or wild animals or, well, whatever else there might have been, leaves and seeds had blown in and then came the monsoon rains. So now there was a spreading of mixed weeds and a few creepers had started adventuring about, climbing up the chairs and tables. Birds had come after honey or berries and mice or rats had been at the upholstery. Very comfortable, those chairs had been when I was waiting around, hoping that someone would be induced to see sense. But they never did see it; they were so deep in the security of making money, just as Lily had been deep in music; so that nothing else seemed to get through. And I had my Christmas present for Lily on my knee. So beautifully packaged; I remember that.

We looked into that very delightful informal restaurant – you didn't even have to wear a tie – facing on to the garden that had been so delicately landscaped by a Chinese expert. He would have been furious at the big weeds swarming over his dwarf trees. Here the plants and their animal followers had just walked in over the sills. There were even some wild orchids among them, the little white ones. That was the table where Lily and I used to eat salads and fruit and talk about – yes, probably, ourselves. But the ceramics, the bright silver and brass work, the linens, the sharp light on the wine glass, the flimsy pretty curtains and lampshades, where were they? Nowhere for Lily and me, not a chair whole or clean. I caught Salim watching me. But perhaps it was not out of unkindness or suspicion.

We found our way up the stairs. They were not very grand, for of course everyone used the lifts, half a dozen of them there had been, always bright and polished when you stepped in, and a smiling lift-boy to be tipped later – if one remembered. I thought of forcing open one of the shut, dark doors, just to see, but then decided not to. The first landing was astonishingly overgrown and one corner heaped with a huge fungus that appeared to be housing quite a population of little nasties. Once the windows were gone it was easy for all sorts of spores to drift in and settle cosily. The floor covering had rotted away as quickly as if it had been pieces of dead wood on a rain-forest floor.

Perhaps it was as well that things did rot. I found my first casualty on that floor with a knife still in his ribs. Or perhaps hers. Salim looked at it coldly. The flesh had been very tidily eaten away, probably by rats, though something larger had been at the long bones. There were a few tatters of cloth. Probably a man, but his wallet had been gnawed, except for the metal clip – gold, was it? – so that I wasn't able to make a guess at who it had been. I couldn't help hoping that the flesh-eaters had made as good a job of other corpses.

We unlocked two or three doors and went into another room where the door had been left open and had swung so violently that it was half off its hinges, the pre-monsoon winds, I expect. These had been air-conditioned rooms and on the whole the windows were still shut. But patches of fungus had spread; some of the bathrooms were thick with it. The room with the open door had been cleared out, but the others had plenty of evidence; one, even, had the beginning of a letter on a neat little typewriter. I stopped long enough to make notes, but the atmosphere was unpleasant. The rooms had of course heated up during the hot weather of two years, with no air condition-ing. I felt choked. In several I noticed bottles intact, a discreet breaking of the laws which were enforced against the poor. I found it had mixed associations for me: some rather powerful. Salim always tells me to cut that out. It is easy for him, engrossed in his present and possible future.

Our assignment had been just to get an idea of what had happened in the city during the two years. The events of the first three months were sufficiently well known and documented. In fact, there were far too many photographs; almost everyone either had a camera or quickly looted one. But after that, with the specific weapons of the counter-attacking forces causing complete withdrawal from the city which, how-ever, was by now lethal to its new conquerors, nobody quite knew what was what, only that the counter-attack had petered out. World developments elsewhere had seen to that.

So now it was important to make an assessment of the city. If buildings were in reasonably good condition they might be re-used. Possible uses had not yet been considered in detail, but that would certainly be on the immediate agenda.

We next took a look at the swimming pool, which was on the first-floor level, partly over the garden-view restaurant. I had not much wanted to do this in case there were remains. At one point several men and women, deservedly in a way, had been taken, condemned, tied and thrown into the pool. I had known some of them and though the relationship had been one of irritation and anger I still did not relish this kind of confrontation. But that had been cleared up; the bodies, Salim said, had been fished out and taken to the mass grave in the Botanical Gardens. After that the water had partially evaporated in the hot weather, since the circulating and purifying mechanism had of course stopped; but the pool had filled again in the rains. Yet it was totally changed; leaves had drifted in and rotted; there was an abundance of larval life in the brownish shallows, where the shining blue tiles were almost obliterated. 'We should get some fish to clean this up,' I said to Salim, 'otherwise malaria will spread.'

Salim said doubtfully that he would try. I believe he is doing this now. One interesting thing was that seeds had blown in from the slight overhang of the next-door trees and there were healthy saplings already prising up the mosaic where the chaises-longues and little tables had been, with young men like Salim scurrying about with drinks and sandwiches and ice-creams, accepting tips but thinking – what? Well, one knew now. The umbrellas had all blown away, but some of their stands were still there. Wicker chairs, too, had blown into a corner, become overgrown and now had birds nesting in them; the wicker had blended in better than rusting metal and plastics. There were ingenious spiders' webs, too, and bright metallic-looking beetles picking up a living. Quite a take-over.

We had to go on to the upper floors. It was much the same, except that twice we came on corpses inside locked rooms and they were totally unpleasant, not having been cleaned up by predators. The smell was terrible until we had smashed some windows. Salim was making a list of useful consumer goods from pencils and torches and gift packages of soap to spectacles and watches and on to radios, tellies, typewriters and computers. There was clothing still hanging in some of the wardrobes, but we agreed that the smell of mildew, and worse, made them unacceptable except as waste for processing. On the upper floors the windows could be opened. Sometimes an adventurous creeper had got this far. One couldn't help a slight feeling of applause. Good luck to them!

And so we came to the room I was afraid of. I had the key, but it was not locked and it did not have what had been burning in me since I volunteered for this particular mission. In fact the room was tidy; the violin was in its case. Salim made a note of it; he had never seen one close. I explained that the damp and heat would have affected the strings and probably warped the body, but this could perhaps be restored. The body looked all right; it had survived almost three centuries, though in a cooler climate. Salim touched this thing from Europe gently. I was trying not to think of her hand, her cheek, her shoulder. The piles of music seemed to be only slightly mildewed and frayed at the edges; the same with the books, and all the little things she couldn't travel without. There was a scent bottle there, half full. It would have been terrible to open it. And know. And know. Beside it was a letter from her agent about an American contract. I looked at the date. Yes, it was the week before when I had been trying hard to warn her. Apparently she had answered it. If only she had left then. If only. But she hated being hurried, wouldn't take me seriously.

The letter to me. I had half expected it. Yet, when I saw it propped against the mirror which by now was blotched, but still unbroken, I found it difficult to keep my hand steady. I am not sure how much Salim knew. Probably something, but his and my definitions of love would be strangely different, more so than our definitions of justice. She wrote that yes, I had been right and she had been silly, hadn't she, but now it was too late and if I ever found this letter I was not to be sad or angry. She was going down to sit somewhere among the flowers and when she heard the shooting coming close she would take enough of her sleeping pills. This of course had been written after the fatal 11 a.m., though she had not dated it. The television set in the room had been left on, though now it was blank. I wondered what had been the last thing shown on it. I folded the letter and stood looking out of the window. Which flowers? Perhaps in front among the alamandas and tall fuchsias, the ipomeas and jasmines which were going to be set free. She had always enjoyed sitting there watching the traffic, so varied and brightly coloured, from the front row of the dress circle, so to speak. Laughing about it. A few days must have gone by while her body still sat there, her scarf still blown in the broken sunlight. Then all corpses had been cleared from the streets, thrown into trucks and taken to the Botanical Gardens.

When I turned round Salim had opened the sliding doors of the cupboard. What I found it hard to take was not so much the dresses and the furs, but the row of shoes. They seemed to be waiting. I went out very quickly. I had not even looked to see if she had left any of her jewellery. If so Salim would have taken it out, carefully noted down everything and as carefully handed it all over to the correct official body in the Department, for ultimate sale. That is something I do not want to know about. The letter ended with love and a little laughing and remembering. She must have gone to sleep among those flowers, those plants which were going to win, to take over from us humans.

We spent the whole day going over the hotel, making notes, not speaking to one another too loudly, and then suddenly it was night. I think somehow we had both irrationally expected that the lights would go on, and though we knew perfectly well that nothing of the kind could happen, yet we were surprised and rather upset. We decided not to go back but to bed down on the comfortable banquettes in the main reception area. Neither of us felt like going into a bedroom. We opened a couple of tins and bottles of soda water, gone rather stale. It was perhaps simpler for Salim than for me: we had won, that was good. I kept a question mark over both; it was only that we'd had the same enemy. Was that enough? I didn't know, only I was sure I did not feel like a winner. But over exactly who or what – now? When we lay down there were constant small rustlings and a strong smell of jasmine, perhaps also something sharper and earthier, but certainly a plant. Whoever else had won, they had. Later the moon rose and its light came filtering down on to us through thousands of eager and growing leaves. Forcing and teasing and tearing their way into what had been human territory, but would soon be theirs.

BIOGRAPHICAL NOTes

KIRKPATRICK DOBIE was born in Dumfries in 1908. His work has appeared in earlier volumes of *Scottish Short Stories*, but he is known chiefly for his collections of poetry: *A Fatal Tree*, 1971; *Like Tracks of Birds*, 1976; *That Other Life*, 1980; *Poems from a Provincial Town*, 1983; *Against the Tide*, 1985. He is a retired grain merchant.

ROSA MACPHERSON was born in Alloa in 1956 of mid-European parents. She has published stories in the *Edinburgh Review* and in *New Writing Scotland*, and she is tutor for the Alloa Writers' Group.

GEORGE MACKAY BROWN has always lived in Orkney. He has published seven collections of poems (most recently, *Christmas Poems*, 1984), three novels (including *Time in a Red Coat*, 1984), three books of legends and stories for young people, two collections of short stories (*Andrina*, 1983, and *Christmas Stories*, 1985) and several plays. He has numerous other literary projects in various stages of completion.

ERIK COUTTS was born in 1942 in Aberdeenshire, and was educated in Aberdeen, where he qualified in agriculture, since when he has spent most of his life farming. He has two children.

LORN MACINTYRE was born in Argyll. A full-time writer, he now lives near St Andrews.

JANE WEBSTER was born in Edinburgh in 1956. After studying English at Stirling University, she worked for some years as a theatre technician, then as a social worker. She writes poetry and short stories.

IAN RANKIN was born in Cardenden, Fife, in 1960, and went to Edinburgh University. His short stories have appeared in the *Edinburgh Review*, *Cencrastus*, the *Scottish Review*, *New Writing Scotland* 2 and 3, and have been broadcast on Radio 4. His first novel, *The Flood*, was published by Polygon in 1986, and his second, *Knots and Crosses*, by the Bodley Head in 1987.

MAUREEN MONAGHAN was born in Glasgow and educated there and in Ayrshire. After many years as a teacher, she gave it up to open a small restaurant with her husband. She started writing fairly recently; her first story was published in the collection, *The Other Side of the Clyde*, and since then she has continued to write stories and poems, and is planning a novel.

PETER REGENT was born in Suffolk and educated in Norfolk and at Oxford. He has now lived in Fife for more than twenty years. His collection of short stories, *Laughing Pig*, was published by Robin Clark in 1984.

ANDREW COWAN is twenty-five. He has recently completed an MA in Creative Writing at the University of East Anglia, and is currently working to establish an oral history project in Norwich, where he lives.

JACKSON WEBB was born in Colorado and has lived in Galloway for the past twelve years. His stories have appeared on Radio 3 and in Scottish Arts Council collections, *Words*, *Blackwood's*, *New Writing Scotland* 1983 and 1984, and the *Scottish Review*. His first book, *The Last Lemon Grove* (Weidenfeld), was chosen by George Mackay Brown as the *Scotsman*'s Book of the Year. He received the Tom-Gallon Award, a Scottish Arts Council Bursary, in 1981, has been tutor for the Galloway and Skye Writers' Workshop, and was Writer-in-Residence for Yorkshire Arts in 1983–4. His two recently finished works, *The Events on Isikos* (a novel) and *Drumfern Almanac*, have received the Yorkshire Arts Award.

RONALD FRAME was born in 1953 in Glasgow, and educated there and at Oxford. He is the author of four books of fiction, all published by the Bodley Head: *Winter Journey*, *Watching Mrs Gordon*, *A Long Weekend with Marcel Proust* and *Sandmouth People*. He has finished work on a fifth. He shared the first Betty Trask prize for fiction. Last year his first radio play was nominated for the Sony Awards, and he won the Samuel Beckett Award for the best first television play (*Paris*) and Pye's Most Promising Writer New to Television category.

CHRISTINE ADAM was born in Paisley in 1952. She studied Philosophy at the University of Glasgow, and since then has had a wide variety of jobs, none of which required a degree in anything. She now lives in Edinburgh with her husband and son and the first twenty pages of a novel.

MAEVE McDOWALL was born in Ireland and brought up in England. She has lived in Scotland since graduating from St Andrews University and she now works in education. She is married with two sons.

GUY KENNAWAY is twenty-nine. He went to Edinburgh University, and subsequently published two novels, *I Can Feel It Moving* (1984) and *The Winner of the Fooker Prize* (1985), both with Quartet. He is now working on some film scripts.

PHILIP HOBSBAUM has taught at the University of Glasgow since 1966 and is now Titular Professor of English Literature there. He has published four collections of poems and one of his short stories appeared in the 1977 edition of *Scottish Short Stories*. Recent publications include *A Reader's Guide to D. H. Lawrence* and *Essentials of Literary Criticism*. He is working on a study of Robert Lowell.

ASTRID WILSON was born in 1941 and educated in Edinburgh. She studied English at university there, and then studied film at University College London. In 1982 she gave up teaching in order to be able to write full time. She now lives in London.

NAOMI MICHISON was born in 1897 and educated at Oxford. Originally interested in the classical period, then in Scotland, later in Africa, she has written some seventy books, ranging from novels as famous as *The Corn King and the Spring Queen* to a recent volume of stories about the Neolithic settlers on Orkney. Her memoir, *You May Well Ask*, has just been reissued by Fontana Paperbacks. She has five children and an ever-growing number of grandchildren and great-grandchildren, and she divides her time between her farm in Carradale, Argyll, and London and Botswana.